"What about me and my peace of mind?"

Penny kept her voice deliberately soft. "Do you expect me to sit back and smile when my father moves from one life-risking adventure to another? Am I supposed to clink glasses with you and say, 'Here's hoping he makes it out alive this time?' Steffan, don't I count?"

"You count very much." He lifted one hand to stroke her hair slowly, and she sensed an overpowering tenderness in his touch. "But I can't allow my feelings for you to pressure me into an unfair decision."

She didn't want to quarrel with him. She wanted to glide into the circle of his arms and stay there, to feel his breath on her ear as he whispered reassurances. But he was wrong. So wrong. "Please."

"I can't."

Virginia Hart comes from a family of writers. Her sister writes mysteries, and her husband—who's even more romantic than Virginia's heroes—is an award-winning country music songwriter. Virginia, not to be outdone, has written mysteries, historical romances, Westerns, and now Harlequin Romances. Confusion is the order of the day at the Harts' Burbank, California, home, with Virginia at her typewriter, cola in hand—she says she's addicted—and her husband composing and singing at the top of his lungs. Their two sons, no doubt, add to the creative chaos.

Books by Virginia Hart

WITHOUT RAINBOWS

Virginia Hart

Harlequin Books

TORONTO • NEW YORK • LONDON
AMSTERDAM • PARIS • SYDNEY • HAMBURG
STOCKHOLM • ATHENS • TOKYO • MILAN

ISBN 0-373-02980-2

Harlequin Romance first edition May 1989

Printed in U.S.A.

CHAPTER ONE

As she hurried down the cool dark corridor, her steps soundless on the grass-green carpet, Penny Haywood felt as if she were an observer in someone else's unwelcome dream.

Through the wide-flung glass doors, she caught sight of her father, having lunch on the terrace as if nothing had happened. Seized by a mixture of disbelief and outrage, she drew a sharp breath and stopped walking.

The woman who led the way eyed her quizzically and stopped, too. "Is something wrong?"

Wrong? Penny had an impulse to laugh. No, everything was idyllic.

Could so much actually have happened in three days? Was she truly in Greece again? Or would her clock-radio alarm go off at any moment with the weather report and the latest on freeway-traffic conditions?

It had all begun less than two days earlier, with a telegram in the middle of the night, informing her that her father had been injured in a fall from a mountain somewhere in Peru.

"Peru?" Penny had echoed aloud, though she'd been alone. Her mind was snagged on the image of her father's brush with death in such a faraway-sounding place.

Hoping there had been some mistake, perhaps a mix-up of identities, she'd immediately called the house in Athens that was his home base and let the phone ring for a very long time. But there was no answer

Frantic calls to Peru to get more information on the accident were fruitless. Her Spanish was sketchy at best, long-distance connections were poor, and no one at the office where the wire originated seemed to know anything about the physical condition or whereabouts of Lon Haywood.

When she'd almost gone out of her mind with worry, the phone rang. The woman who called, identifying herself as Wanda Rice, was reluctant at first to discuss details.

"Lon was on one of his treasure digs in Peru," she explained matter-of-factly, as she might have reported that he'd slipped on a cake of soap in the bathtub. "The find was bigger than he'd anticipated—mostly Spanish gold coins— and his partners got greedy. Those two were pretty seamy characters. They struck him on the head and pushed him down the slope, leaving him for dead. Then they disappeared with the loot."

Penny had clutched the telephone with both hands, her gasp inaudible.

"Fortunately he'd made friends with a Peruvian family who sent someone to search for him when they suspected foul play. It was the oldest son who sent you the wire. He shouldn't have. It probably scared the daylights out of you."

"My father," Penny broke in, not wanting to hear anything else until she knew the worst. "How badly hurt is he?"

"He'll be fine. In fact, he's back here in Athens."

"That's not possible. I tried the house again and again."

"He's not at his own place," the woman explained. "He's at the Korda villa, recuperating. That's all I can say right now. Lon would have my head if he knew I told you this much."

"The Korda villa? Was Steffan Korda a part of this?"

The woman hesitated. "I really can't say."

She didn't have to. Steffan had probably helped finance the ill-fated venture. He'd done it before. But he'd never gone along on any of them, never taken any of the risks.

Tearing her attention away from the telephone, Penny had glanced at the clock for the first time in hours. She'd been so distraught she hardly knew if it was day or night. "I'll call the airlines and see about a flight as soon as I hang up."

"It really isn't necessary for you to drop everything and fly here. Wouldn't it be better to wait a month or so until the chaos dies down? Then you and your father could have a fun visit."

A fun visit? The unlikely suggestion had given Penny a moment's pause. Who was this woman? If she was close enough to Lon to assume the task of calling his daughter about the accident, why hadn't he mentioned her in any of his letters?

Or had he?

Was Wanda the "friend" he'd written about, the friend who loved Greece and had decided to stay but was having difficulty with the language? Penny would find out before long.

"I'll be there as soon as I can arrange it," she'd promised. "Thank you for calling."

The hectic preparations—securing an extended leave of absence from her job, making travel plans and crying down her mother's objections—had kept her too busy to do much worrying. But later, the interminable delays, the long flight, and the snarl of Athens traffic, like no other traffic in the world, had given her time to conjure up the worst.

If her father was truly all right, why was he now staying with Steffan Korda? He was a man who preferred looking after himself when he was ill. Would he be horribly injured, then? Scarred? Had her caller played down the severity of the accident to keep her from losing control? Would Penny be able to keep from crying out when she saw him?

"Penelope?" It was Wanda Rice, the woman who'd called her in St. Louis, then picked her up at the airport. They hadn't spoken much during the drive, but now she put a tentative hand on Penny's shoulder. Penny looked at her dispassionately. Slim-hipped, with glossy, midlength chestnut hair, Wanda was attractive, if not beautiful, in a tanned athletic way.

"Penelope," she said again, "can you be calm and collected when we go out there and face Lon? For my sake? Don't let on I told you about what happened on that mountain."

"How can I possibly be calm?"

"I don't know." The woman's laugh was throaty. "Think green trees and sunshine."

"If I'm not supposed to know he's been hurt, how did you explain my coming here?"

"You've been writing on and off that you planned to visit, haven't you?" Wanda shrugged one shoulder. "He thinks it's a coincidence. Your pa's a great believer in the vicissitudes of fate."

"Fate?" Penny repeated. How did the woman know what she'd written in her letters? Had Lon shared them with her? The thought wasn't very comforting.

Bright summer flowers grew in planned profusion in the lemony sunlight, giving the terrace the shimmering look of a Renoir painting. Lon Haywood, who was enjoying a gigantic fruit salad, spotted his daughter, dropped his napkin in his plate and rose unsteadily. "Penny, darlin'."

His features weren't pain-twisted. His eyes weren't sunken. He wasn't even string-bean thin. He wore his hair longish now. Father and daughter might have visited the same barber, she thought wryly, regretting again the impulsive decision to have her sun-streaked ash-blond hair cropped close to frame her oval face with a cap of gentle curls.

Aside from the cast on one arm and a slight drawing down of one eye because of an already healing gash beneath it, he looked remarkably young and fit, very much the same as he had looked when she'd last seen him, nine years ago. If he'd appeared more pitiful, she might have been able to excuse his breezy, things-could-be-better grin. Instead, prickles of anger began working at the nape of her neck as she remembered other foolhardy escapades that had nearly lost her a father.

An old silver-mine shaft in Colorado had collapsed when Penny was ten, burying Lon and his companions for thirty-six hours. One of his crew hadn't made it. A year later, his diving equipment failed when he was checking out a wreck in Bermuda waters, and he'd almost drowned. How many other narrow escapes had there been that she didn't even know about? It had to end here. Now. The fun was over. It wasn't a game anymore. He'd risked his life one too many times.

"Hello, Daddy," she said, wishing at once that the "Daddy" hadn't slipped out. Addressing him as "Father" would have been more appropriate to her state of mind.

"What's wrong, baby?" he cocked his head stiffly to one side. "No kiss for the old man?"

She sighed. Did anything ever change? How many times had he come home after being away for weeks, trying to raise some sunken galleon in the Florida Keys or searching for the Seven Cities of Cibola, and said that very thing? How many times had her irritation melted, as it was melting now?

She started toward him, slowly at first, then faster, until she was clasped in the circle of his good arm. Accepting his brief hard kiss gratefully, she nuzzled against his chest. He gasped in pain and she drew back with an outcry of her own. His middle was heavily taped. She could feel the bandages through his shirt. The discovery brought back all the fears and uncertainties of the past few days, and she had to clasp her hands tightly together to keep them from trembling.

"You've grown into a real beauty, hasn't she, Wanda?" Lon asked, pretending not to notice his daughter's reaction.

"She's an extremely attractive young woman," Wanda said dutifully, setting onto a chaise longue that was shaped like half a giant bean pod. Snatching up a magazine, she began to fan herself furiously.

"Sit down, baby." Lon made a wide gesture toward Penny with his free hand. "Have something cold to drink and tell me what you've been up to."

"I believe you should tell me what *you've* been up to," she countered.

"You mean...this?" He lowered himself into his chair with an ill-controlled grimace and indicated the bandaged arm as if he'd only just noticed it himself. "I'll tell you about it later."

"I'd like to hear about it now."

"I took a tumble. It was nothing."

"You're bound up head to toe—like a mummy—and it's nothing?" Penny scraped a chair close to his and sat down, placing her handbag on the floor. "What happened?"

"Your dad is getting clumsy in his old age."

It was an opening she couldn't afford to let slip by. "So you're willing to admit you aren't twenty-five anymore. The next step is to admit that it's time you settled down and led a normal life."

Lon outlined the rim of his glass with an index finger. "Normal. By whose standards?"

"You didn't end up in that condition by falling out of bed," Penny insisted. "You might as well tell me about it. I don't intend to be put off."

"No doubt about it, Lon. Your little girl is a woman. She's not back five minutes, and already she's begun her cross-examination."

If Steffan Korda had been there when she'd arrived, she hadn't noticed him. Settled comfortably in a high-backed wicker chair, he regarded Penny with amusement. The years hadn't changed him, any more than they'd changed Lon. Penny stared, in a kind of shocked recognition, at his glistening black eyes, his slow-spreading smile, the black peaks of his eyebrows.

He was teasing her. But he was teasing in earnest. And he was right, she told herself briskly. She'd landed on her father with both feet. It would have been far better had she allowed them a bit of getting-acquainted time first.

"Well, you two," Lon said quickly, using the interruption to distract her, "I don't suppose introductions are necessary."

"Certainly not. We're old friends." Steffan raised his glass in a salute. "Tell me, Penny, do you plan to rebuild your nest in the pear tree? Or will you begin a new one?"

"What's this about a nest?" Wanda looked up from the magazine she'd been reading.

Penny's confidence skidded several notches. Why did he have to remember her tree-climbing, of all things?

In this section of the city, sprawling villas often sat beside modest dwellings. The Haywoods had lived just next door to the Kordas—if it could properly be called "next door." The houses had been separated by a terraced slope, a swimming pool, tennis courts and guest quarters.

Elegant parties were frequent then, when Basil Korda, Steffan's father, was alive. In her early teen years, wanting to spy on the comings and goings of her glamorous neighbors, Penny had often armed herself with binoculars and taken a perch in the fork of a tree that sat just over the property line.

One day Steffan spotted her. When he helped her down, she stammered out a story about being a bird-watcher. Perhaps he didn't believe her, but he was polite enough to pretend he did, and she was totally captivated by his striking good looks and his gallantry.

From then on, whenever their paths crossed—as often as she could "accidently" bump into him—she fed him bits of bird lore gleaned from an encyclopedia, and he'd dubbed her "Sparrow."

Did he remember that, too?

"I haven't made any definite plans yet," Penny said vaguely, hoping to avoid any more references to nests or birds. And hoping her bright smile would hide her embarrassment.

"But getting your father to toe the mark appears to be first on the agenda."

She bit back a snappish retort. He was being protective of his friend, after all, and she couldn't fault him for that. Besides, she didn't want to make an enemy of him. She had to admit she was still strongly attracted to him; not only that, she needed his help. If anyone could convince Lon to start behaving like a grown-up, it was Steffan.

"I wouldn't be much of a daughter if I weren't concerned for his safety."

"And you wouldn't be much of a woman if you didn't try to reform him."

Another slap at womanhood. It was uttered with the same smile, but it was a slap nonetheless. She couldn't ignore it.

"How many bones have you broken lately, Steffan?" she asked. "Or do you only sit back and enjoy other men's adventures vicariously?" *As your father did before you*, she might have added, but didn't, in deference to his father's not being there to defend himself.

Her remark seemed to wash over him unnoticed. "My way of life is somewhat dull by comparison."

"But you aren't planning to trade in your briefcase for a diving suit or a metal detector, are you?"

Lon guffawed,and smacked the glass-topped table with one hand. "She's something, isn't she? You know, when she was a little kid, I used to think how sad it was. She had a pretty woman like Constance for a mother and had to take after me. But damned if she didn't survive the resemblance. I can't get over the way she turned out."

"She has more than a little of her mother in her," Steffan said, measuring his words in a way that let Penny know two things. One, he had noticed her questions and taken offense at them. Two, he disliked her mother as much as her mother disliked him and all the Kordas.

Constance Haywood had always placed the blame for the failure of her marriage to Lon, and their eventual divorce, at Basil Korda's feet. Basil had once been a salvager of sunken vessels and a tracer of lost gold mines. Against all odds, the family fortune had begun with such unlikely ventures. Wise investments that brought about his ownership of a chain of luxurious hotels had done the rest. But there was nothing thrilling in tales of the stock market and land speculation, so all that had been brushed aside.

Basil's rags-to-riches boasting had made Lon dissatisfied with his well-paying but ordinary sales job in a cousin's business-machine company. He wasn't inspired by the promise that expansion and his cousin's eventual relocation to the south of France would leave him in full charge of a growing firm. Calculators and computers were not the things his dreams were made of.

Basil was dead now. According to one of Lon's letters, he'd suffered a heart attack a little over two years ago while presiding over a stockholders' meeting. But Steffan appeared to be following in his footsteps; the letters hinted that he encouraged Lon, and sometimes even helped finance his get-rich-quick madness.

"How's Constance?" Lon asked, jovially missing the undercurrent in the exchange. "Busy as ever, is she?"

"She's selling the shop and taking a trip soon," Penny said, the skin beneath her linen dress warming uncomfortably under Steffan's unflinching scrutiny.

The air was dry in Greece, she reminded herself irritably. People seldom perspired. Besides, she wasn't fifteen anymore and he hadn't caught her in his pear tree. She'd always prided herself on her ability to stay cool and poised under the most trying of circumstances.

"Your mom never was one to travel," her father was saying.

"She isn't usually. But she's going to Hawaii to ponder an important decision. She may marry again."

There. She'd said it. Would it be too obvious to bring out the snapshots of her mother she'd slipped into her handbag, hoping to jog his memory of the woman he'd married, and the good times they'd shared?

Lon blinked. "I wish her every happiness. God knows, she deserves it." Was there regret in his voice? Jealousy? She hoped so.

"As I said," she added quickly, not wanting him to accept the possible marriage as fact, "She isn't certain yet. She only—"

"*Signomi*, Kyrie Haywood." The maid, an attractive dark-haired girl in a silky gray dress, had appeared in the doorway. "The doctor is here."

Lon snapped his fingers. "I forgot. Show him into the library, will you, honey?"

Wanda was on her feet as he attempted to rise. "Let me help you."

"Don't mother me, Wanda." He brushed away her efforts with impatience. "I'm not an invalid."

"Don't be so obstinate." She gripped one arm firmly and, despite his protests, moved with him. This time he offered no objections.

"Don't go away, baby." He stopped briefly by the door and pointed a finger at Penny. "This won't take a minute."

A delicious breeze rippled through the surrounding trees, bringing with it the heady scent of orange blossoms, pine, jasmine—and the sea. A scent that was Greece. Penny inhaled deeply, remembering.

She hadn't fully realized until that moment that she was here. Really here. Glyfada, a suburb of Athens, had been her home, after all, through most of her growing-up years.

She'd been born in St. Louis, Missouri, of parents who were also born there. But when she was four, her father's Aunt Penelope died. Actually she was his great-aunt, his grandfather's sister on his mother's side, and one of the few members of the family that still remained in Greece. The only girl in a family of boys, Aunt Penelope had been expected to act as nurse, cook and housekeeper. She had never married and regretted having no children of her own.

She'd taken a great fancy to Lon when he'd stopped off for visits on his way to one adventure or another. Touched when he named his only daughter after her, she'd left him her house.

The idea of living in Greece, the land of his roots, appealed to Lon's sense of excitement. Constance was enthusiastic about the move, too, seeing in it a chance to wrench him away from the influence of his entourage of worthless friends. And she'd persuaded him to accept the job with his cousin's company—a career with a future.

Penny had loved the house at first sight, though it was little more than a cottage. She'd loved to scramble up the gentle pine-clad slopes and down to the sandy beaches. She'd loved the astonishing friendliness of the people, too.

She didn't mind the often white-hot Athens sun, or even her enforced midday nap. Here, the afternoon rest period was observed by nearly everyone. Mornings began early and nights were long and filled with bustle, noise and excitement.

She'd adored the wonderful ruins she could explore. Ruins that looked like pages out of storybooks and were perfect for games of "let's pretend." But most of all, she adored the tales her newly acquired friends told about gods who were like men, and yet, not like men. Tales that leapt out at her with every step she took, every stone she uncovered.

This reunion with Steffan Korda had been a disappointment and the end of her most recurrent girlhood fantasy. He was supposed to jump up and kiss her hand, then marvel at the desirable woman the scrawny little girl had become. He was supposed to suggest that sometime soon they go for a drive and perhaps for a late supper at an elegant restaurant overlooking the sea. Then over glasses of wine, she would speak to him of her worry about her father's future and he would offer his sympathy and his help.

Hah!

It was a dream to rival the tale of Athena springing fully grown from her father's head.

Suddenly she wanted to leave. To thank her host for his hospitality, take her father and be gone! Another day, when she wasn't so travel-weary, she'd face Steffan again and perhaps win him over.

But not now.

Tonight she'd stretch out on the lumpy, too-soft mattress in her old room and listen to the scritching sound the acacia branches made against the side of the house when the wind blew. The thought of it cheered her.

"How long will you be with us, Penny?" Steffan asked, breaking the long heavy silence they'd shared since Lon left.

Us? Was he deliberately trying to make her feel like an outsider, or was she being oversensitive?

"I'm not sure. As long as my father needs me."

"Ah, I see." His smile deepened, making his eyes crinkle in a way that had once made her heart beat out of rhythm.

Now it only ruffled her. "Did I say something amusing?"

"It's only that a woman always thinks a man needs to be cared for. As if he were—what is the saying? Only a small boy grown tall?"

"In many cases, he is."

He leaned forward. "Would you say that description fits me?"

She mimicked his smile. "No. It would be my guess that you were never a little boy."

His jaw jutted forward as the smile faded. Had she struck a nerve? She hoped so. "I imagine I must seem quite ancient to you. How old are you now? Nineteen? Twenty?"

"I'm twenty-five."

"You seem—" he fluttered one hand "—younger."

So much for the shockingly expensive dress she'd bought for this occasion, thinking its elegant lines made her look more worldly and sophisticated. It was the little-boy haircut. It had to be the haircut. "And how old are you, Steffan?" she threw at him.

A six or seven beat pause preceded his answer. "I'm thirty-five."

"Really? I would have guessed you were older." It wasn't true. She knew Steffan's age exactly. There were ten years and three months between them. In the old days, she'd been the world's expert on Korda trivia.

Possibly guessing that his proximity would have an inhibiting effect, he crossed to take a seat opposite her at the table. "You know you're welcome here, Penny. I only asked about the length of your stay because, if you're going to be in Athens for some time, you might be considering temporary employment."

It was a sensible explanation. There was nothing wrong with the words or with their delivery, yet her scalp tingled with restrained antagonism. "I might."

"You were a bookkeeper in St. Louis?"

"I was—am—assistant advertising manager for the Halver-Knox department stores."

"Advertising," he mused, pushing out the delectable lower lip she'd so often dreamed of kissing. "You found it interesting?"

"Very." A kiss could be truly pleasurable only if two people genuinely liked and respected one another, she reminded herself when her breathing shallowed.

His hand snaked forward and she yanked hers back, scowling, thinking in that brief moment that he planned to touch her. She should have known better. To her chagrin, he was reaching for one of the *loukoumades* from the platter of assorted pastries Lon had left on his lunch tray.

Easily reading her reaction, his eyes crinkled again with merriment as he gestured, eyebrows raised, toward the remaining pastries.

"No?" he questioned, when she shook her head, at his offer. "You don't know what you're missing."

Eating with wholehearted enthusiasm, he expounded on the culinary abilities of their cook and explained what went into the dough as precisely as if he'd done the baking himself.

His was a mobile face, given to switching from frowns to dazzling smiles in a matter of seconds, and without apparent reason. His hands moved in lively accompaniment—smoothing the air in front of him, chopping, waving, and finally twining quietly on the tabletop.

"I've recently opened an office here at the house," he said, serious again. "Wanda's been acting as my secretary. But the work involves more hours than she bargained for, especially now with Lon recuperating from his injuries. She'd rather be available to drive him where he wants to go, run errands for him, or simply be there to keep him from getting too restless since his activities have been restricted."

"I see." And why did Steffan suppose *she* had come all this way? To watch someone else do everything for her father?

"So, if you take dictation," he said, finally getting to the point, "I might be able to use you."

Having Steffan for an employer? Sharpening his pencils and serving him coffee? Calling him "sir"? Not likely.

"I don't," she said.

"Do you type?" Now his expression was one of extreme patience.

If she said no, would he ask if she could read? "Don't worry about me, Steffan," she said with a toss of her head that would have been far more effective if her hair were still shoulder-length. "If I decide to look for work, I won't have any trouble. I'm good at what I do."

Let him chew on that bit of boasting for a while. She *had* made plans. Tentative ones. Sun Dial Sportswear, a St. Louis-based firm that did a lot of business with Halver-Knox, had an affiliate in Athens. Her employer had given her a few names and promised to make the right phone calls should she feel the need to remain with her father for some time.

"It could still be difficult for you," Steffan said. "There are tedious legal technicalities for an American wanting to work in Greece. Logically all of that should have been taken care of while you were still in the States."

"Logically," she repeated, "I didn't have enough warning to deal with the red tape."

"Which is one reason I've invited you to work here. I can smooth the way for you quite easily, and there's more challenge in the hotel business than you'd imagine." His eyes rested on her mouth long enough to make her wonder if her lipstick was smeared. "Possibly even a career. Your advertising background could be an asset to our public-relations department. I only mentioned the clerical skills because working as my secretary would allow you an opportunity to familiarize yourself with the operation."

She'd been wrong about his face. It wasn't the perfect face of a mythological Greek God. The Korda jawline, inherited from his father, was too square. The nose was too pronounced. And the brow, in repose, was a bit furrowed. Then why did the irregularities of the parts make the whole even more pleasing?

He averted his eyes suddenly and swiped a finger through the circle of moisture left by Lon's glass, and she had to smile. Inadvertently she'd turned the tables, making him uncomfortable with her own scrutiny.

Then he was back to himself again. "Well?" The monosyllabic question was sharp, implying that there could be only one answer.

She'd been wrong about his eyes, too. They weren't black. They only looked it because they were extraordinarily deep set. They were brown, with irises full of orangish lights. Now they had almost a satanic glow.

Penny forced herself not to look at him. "I thought I'd made it clear," she said coolly. "No, thank you. I'll manage."

"I have no doubt you'll manage. From the way you burst in here today, anyone could see you were prepared to take over and right the sinking ship. Though I would have supposed that after being away from your father for so many years, you'd have been more tender in your treatment of him."

"Tender?" she repeated, thinking how foreign the word sounded coming from him.

"Compassionate. Don't you realize he's been through an ordeal that would have killed a lesser man?"

At least they weren't fencing anymore. "How am I to know what he's been through when I've been told little or nothing?"

"You have eyes. Use them. As for the details of his mishap—"

"Mishap? Oh, I like your choice of words."

"As for the details of his mishap, if they're so bloody important to you, you might have the grace to wait until he's prepared to tell you."

Where was her father? He'd said he would be gone for only a moment. That moment had stretched to the breaking point already. From inside she could hear muffled voices and the sound of someone playing Chopin on a piano.

Darn Steffan. When she was thirteen, she'd thought him the most attractive man she'd ever seen. Watching him at tennis, the lean muscles of his arms and legs in full play, his gaze intent as he smashed the ball into his opponent's court as if the fate of the universe depended on his winning, Penny had imagined scenarios starring the two of them that made her blush even now.

But if masculine beauty of form and feature were still his, it no longer mattered. His attitude of smug self-importance made the rest irrelevant.

"Our family problems aren't your concern in any case," she told him.

"Lon is my friend."

"And he's my father." Her voice was becoming shrill. She knew it, but was too incensed to care. "I intend to use this mishap, as you term it, to make him see that he can't waste the rest of his life searching for a pot of gold that isn't there."

"Stop your shrieking." His unexpected snarl silenced her. But only for an instant.

"Goodbye, Steffan." She plucked her handbag from the floor with an exaggerated flourish. "It's been ... well ... interesting."

"Where do you think you're going?"

"Dad and I are going home. Home is right next door, in case you've forgotten."

He shot a glance toward the house and moistened his lower lip with his tongue. "But you are already set up in my guest house."

"I wouldn't dream of imposing."

When he reached out this time, it wasn't for a *loukou made*. He caught her wrist and held it. "I insist you remain here. For tonight at least."

"*You* insist?" She stared at him. Even Steffan Korda couldn't have so much gall.

Her mother hadn't exaggerated. Basil Korda—and now the chip off the old block—were bent on manipulating the lives of all who came into contact with them. It bolstered their gigantic egos to discuss their successes and triumphs with her father, who was too easygoing to suspect their motives.

"I'm sorry," he said, releasing her. He wasn't. But he had the good sense to know he'd gone too far.

"Do you push and pull a client's arm to force him to stay and listen to what you have to say?" she asked. "Or do you only manhandle women?"

He held up his hands and assumed the expression of someone horrendously misjudged. "Penelope, I—"

"Is that how you got where you are?" she cut in. "Oh, no. I forgot. Your father made the money. It was handed to you on a silver platter."

The penitent pose faded quickly as the light went out of his eyes. They were black again—black and threatening.

"Your father isn't well. He needs peace of mind to recuperate."

"I'll see that he gets it, doctor."

"Don't you realize that it won't take much negative talk from the daughter he loves to crush him completely? Didn't he already manage to survive seventeen years of female nagging? Of trying his damnedest to fit into a pattern of life cut out by someone else?"

She wouldn't slap him. She wouldn't. He would love it if she lost control. "Are you referring to the years my mother and father lived together?"

"I thought it was obvious."

She scraped back her chair and stood up. "What I find obvious, Steffan, is that you're a misogynist. I shouldn't take your vitriol to heart. You don't know me, and you don't know my mother."

"I knew her. I saw her in action."

"You didn't live under the same roof with us. How could you feel qualified to judge my parents' marriage?"

He shrugged. "Would I have to be stretched across an anthill to know that it would be an unpleasant experience?"

"Is something up?" Lon's face seemed paler, and his step more uncertain as he came through the double doors to join them. Wanda trailed behind him, reaching out as if she feared he might fall. "Your discussion sounded pretty lively."

"Penny was telling me that she's exhausted," Steffan lied. "Her flight was a tedious one."

"I'm not in the least tired," she protested.

"Of course, you are, baby." Lon slid his arm around her waist. "I was so glad to see you, I didn't think."

"Wanda, why don't you show her to the guest house? I'll have someone bring her bags along." Steffan's calmly voiced suggestion, reinforced by a raised eyebrow, warned the woman to get hopping.

The message was acknowledged with the barest of flickers across Wanda's face. But it was enough to convince Penny that the two were together in this. In what? Protecting Lon from his own daughter? The idea was insulting. Couldn't they understand that her only concern was for his safety?

If they were so protective of him, where had they been when he took off on the ill-fated adventure that nearly lost him his life? Waving goodbye at the airport? Had Steffan slapped her father's two murderous companions on the back and wished them good luck?

"Run along, baby." Lon gave Penny a wink that was designed to be reassuring. "I'll be there before you know it."

She looked from her father to Steffan and back to her father again, torn between her love for Lon and her need for answers. The weariness in the older man's stance decided her.

She'd go. The battle could wait. But oh, there would be a battle to remember. And she was fairly confident of the outcome.

CHAPTER TWO

IT MIGHT HAVE BEEN the cottage found by Hansel and Gretel in their fairy-tale woods. The guest house stood there in a tangle of cerise bougainvillea, the path leading up to the front door arched with white trellises, heavy with purple grapes. Its sparkling white sides looked remarkably like spun sugar and its rusty-tiled roof could easily have been fashioned of gingerbread.

Except the threat wasn't in the guest house. And it didn't come from a witch, but an ogre.

"Lon can't manage the winding staircase in the main house yet," Wanda explained, opening the door. "And he likes his privacy. So Steffan put him back here. The place is larger than it appears at first glance. There are two bedrooms, sitting room, a complete bath and a kitchen. You'll take your meals with Steffan, of course. But you'll want midnight snacks within reach. We keep—that is, er, Lon...is stocked up on cold drinks, tinned soups, crackers. You know, the standard goodies."

We keep... Wanda had started to say. *We*. Penny might have thought nothing of that slip of the tongue if the woman's face hadn't colored, if she hadn't stumbled painfully over the rest of the sentence. Anyone would have guessed long before this that her father and Wanda were a twosome. Why the secrecy? Apparently theirs was more than just a casual relationship, but that wasn't surprising. He could hardly have been expected to go without female companionship all these years.

Was it a relationship that would end in marriage? Penny had her doubts. The woman wasn't his type at all. She was nothing like Constance. Outdoorsy, with a throaty, almost masculine laugh, and a scrubbed tomboy look, she'd be a comfortable companion and a "good sport."

Still, Penny had sensed something else when the two were together. Something she'd supposed was only born out of Wanda's natural concern about Lon's injuries. Now she wondered.

The painting on the wall behind the couch showed a pirate ship giving chase, and firing upon an already-battered vessel. The expression on one of the buccaneers' faces reminded Penny of Steffan and their confrontation of a few moments before.

"Steffan's still living in the Dark Ages," she fumed. "Women are to be ordered about, physically abused, and sent on their way. So the men can sit around the campfire and boast about the day's hunt."

Wanda gave her a tolerant smile. "You know men. *Philatemo.*"

"*Philatemo!*" Penny hooted. As if that explained everything.

The word had no exact equivalent in English. But loosely translated, it means ego, pride, self-love— the need to be right at all times and at all costs. She'd heard it many, many times during her years of living in Athens, usually intended to excuse boorish behavior.

"Steffan takes some getting used to. But he's all right."

"I don't plan to be here long enough to get used to him. We have a perfectly good house of our own and that's where Dad and I belong."

Wanda frowned. Her fingers played absently with the band of her wristwatch. "Hon, will you forget about moving for the time being?"

"If you can give me one sensible reason why I should."

"I can't. Get the story from your pa."

"What story?"

"I really have to go," the woman insisted, almost tripping over a throw rug in her haste to get to the door. "See you later."

"Wait!" Frustrated, Penny watched until Wanda was out of sight. A few seconds later, a balding man with a stiff smile came and silently deposited her bags in the smaller of the two bedrooms.

The heat was oppressive. Lon hadn't turned on the air conditioner. He'd never believed in "manufactured weather," as he called it, and she couldn't determine which of the main switches to turn. She stripped off her dress, then kicked off her shoes and wandered around in her slip, looking for something to read. There were only coin collectors' catalogs, hand-drawn charts, yellowed maps and a shelf full of books about lost silver and gold mines and sailing vessels that had sunk hundreds of years ago. None of it interested her.

The bed looked far more inviting. Despite the argument she'd given her father, she was completely drained. But she wouldn't sleep. She would just stretch out and close her eyes until he came in. Then they'd have their long overdue talk.

Behind closed eyelids, she saw Steffan's handsome but smug face. He was smiling broadly—thinking, no doubt, that he'd put her in her place. When she managed to drive that unwelcome image away, she saw Kenneth Glass, which wasn't much better. Poor Kenneth. He was a nice man. Period. How her mother could even consider marrying him was beyond all reason. It could only have been one last desperate effort to get over her love for Lon.

When Constance Haywood had gathered up her sixteen-year-old daughter and her belongings and left Athens nine years before, she was only hoping to jolt her dreamer husband into realizing how much he would lose if he continued chasing rainbows. The real treasure was already in his possession. A wife who loved him, an adoring daughter and a comfortable home.

The ploy failed. He wrote a letter that would have done credit to William Shakespeare, expressing sorrow at having lost his girls. But glaringly absent were any promises to change. He didn't beg his wife to return and try again. He didn't even suggest it. The letter was postmarked Jamaica.

The smell of coffee nudged her halfway out of the sleep she hadn't planned. Penny could hear someone whispering and opened her eyes. It was dark. At first time and place eluded her. She thought she was in the Colby Avenue apartment she shared with her mother. The people next door were up early and rattling around in their kitchen. The walls were so paper thin, they might have been in the same room. But why were they whispering?

The room was suffocating. She turned over and the light coming through the crack under the door reminded her where she was. The whispering started again. It was her father. Smoothing a damp curl from her forehead, she got up and pulled on her robe.

"Baby!" Lon had the look of a safecracker caught in the act. "What are you doing up?"

Wanda, framed in the doorway of the other bedroom, carried a suitcase. Her hair was covered with a twisted orange scarf and she wasn't wearing any makeup. Another suitcase stood in the middle of the room.

"Taking a trip?" Penny asked, too shocked to be angry.

"Not far." Lon's manner was offhand.

"Far enough to require luggage. How long do you plan to be gone?"

"Only a few days."

"Only a few days." She dug her bare toes into the loopy carpet for control. "I've just got here and you're running off without telling me? Wonderful."

"Don't make it sound like that. Something came up. You were sound asleep and I didn't want to wake you." Lon jerked his head toward the kitchen. "I was leaving you a note."

"How considerate." He'd had time to notify Wanda though, hadn't he? Or had this outing been planned days ago and they'd simply decided not to tell her about it?

"A buddy of mine, Nikko Minotis. He's got troubles and needs my help."

"I see. Have these troubles anything to do with a sunken treasure?"

"Hell, no." Lon guffawed. "Old Nikko doesn't know anything about diving." He squinted at her sideways. "After that long flight, I knew you wouldn't feel like tearing all over the country with me. We're headed for Volos, if you must know."

"Volos? You can't drive that distance in your condition."

Wanda set the suitcase down and came in on cue. "That's why I'm tagging along. To play chauffeur."

The tension in the room threatened to smother them. Her father and Wanda wore matching false smiles, waiting for Penny either to accept their story or scream. The next move was hers.

"Very well. Give me time to get ready," she said calmly.

Obviously Lon hadn't expected that reaction. "Whoa, baby. I can't take you. Your mom would skin me alive if you came down sick."

"I was sitting comfortably in a passenger seat, not flying the airplane. I'm not that fragile."

"This isn't a pleasure trip. We'll be driving straight through."

"I can sleep in the car. Besides, I'm not going along for the scenery."

He pressed his lips together and blew out his cheeks. "Much as I hate to play the heavy right off, I have to give you a firm no on this. Nikko doesn't have much truck with women. Females in their place and all."

"What about Wanda?"

"He knows she has to do the driving. But I can't take you, too. Much as I'd like to. I'll make it up to you. That's a promise."

With a lollipop and a pat on the head? Penny stared at him hard, remembering what her mother had told her before she left.

"Your father is a stranger to you," Constance had said. "You weren't exactly a child when we left, but you hardly ever saw him. He was forever off somewhere."

"Then wouldn't you agree," Penny had asked, "that it's time I got to know my paternal parent?"

"Penny, living under the same roof with your father is no guarantee you'll get to know him. I don't think I ever did."

"But I'm exactly like him. Haven't you told me as much yourself?"

It was true. She was her father's daughter. Everyone said so, and she could see the uncanny resemblance when she went through her treasured horde of photographs. She had his frank, wide-set green eyes, his questioning smile and his tall slender frame. She even had the Haywood nose—straight to the tip, where it tilted unexpectedly upward.

"I only say that when you exasperate me." Constance Haywood had made an admirable try at a smile. "Oh, listen, honey. I'm not trying to turn you against your father. I've always wanted you to love and respect him."

"I know that."

"But you can see him for what he is, can't you? He has absolutely no sense of responsibility. Just because he's been told you're coming doesn't mean he'll be there. Or that he'll stay after you arrive."

It was just as she'd predicted.

Penny looked at her father and held up her hands in defeat. "You win. I'll stay here."

In her tiniest bikini, she would lie on the shimmering sand at the water's edge and let the sun play over her face and warm her body. She'd go into the city, explore some of the shops on Hermes Street and have an ice at a café in Syntagma Square. She'd visit the Parthenon, because no matter how many times a person returned to Athens, such a visit always seemed necessary. Then she would climb Mount Hymettos, as if she were a tourist, and look down at the sprawl of the city, at the changing sea and beyond that to the beckoning mountains of the Peloponnese.

Then she would go home.

Wanda's relief at her surrender was so obvious, she might as well have danced a jig. "Be sure to bring your jacket," she told Lon.

"It's not cold."

"It could turn cold, and you'll be glad you have it. I'll tuck your medication into my overnight bag."

"Why? I'm only supposed to take it if I have pain, and I feel fine," he argued.

"We'd better bring it just in case. I'll put these bags in the trunk."

"Don't forget to leave me the keys." Penny yawned. Maybe she'd climb back into bed and sleep until the next day.

"What keys are those?" Lon asked.

"The keys to the house. *Our* house. I'll go over and get settled while you're away."

"Right." Scowling, he dug into his pockets. "Damn. Now what did I do with those keys?"

"Never mind. I'd be willing to bet you haven't fixed the latch on the kitchen window. I'll climb through the way I used to." The more she considered her plans, the more enthusiastic Penny grew. "If you phone before you start back, I'll have a festive dinner ready. I'm really a very good cook, you know."

"Yeah. Sure." His voice lacked conviction.

"But?"

He snapped his fingers. "The hell with Old Nikko and his outdated hangups about women. Why should I leave my little girl behind just to suit him?"

"Are you saying you want me to come?"

"Damn right. Hustle your bustle though," he prodded, heading for the bathroom. "Time's a-wasting."

"You're coming with us after all?" Wanda asked, returning in time to hear the last of his speech.

"So it seems."

The woman looked at the bathroom door and sidled closer to Penny. "Maybe you'll change your mind when I tell you something. Steffan's flown out already because he had business in Salonika. But he's planning to meet us on Skopelos."

Penny groaned. Skopelos, one of the Sporades islands, was at least four and a half hours by boat once they arrived at Volos. And then she'd be faced with Steffan?

"So 'old Nikko' has problems that require both of them?"

"You've got it."

"Then it's more important than ever that I'm there to see what's going on."

As she took her turn in the bathroom, she could hear Lon in his bedroom, slamming drawers and whistling his favorite song, "When It's Twilight on the Trail." If he was up to something, and she had no doubt he was, why would he agree to take her along? Agree? No. Insist was more like it now.

His problem wasn't hard to figure out. Never one to bother about maintenance, she was willing to bet he'd allowed the house to run down shamefully. Nine years of neglect would have taken their toll. Now he was afraid of Penny's reactions when she saw it.

He should have known better. The condition of the house didn't matter. It was the insulting keep-away tactics he and his coconspirators were using against her that hurt.

Well, the moment of truth couldn't be put off forever, she reminded herself, as she hastily ran a comb through her hair and patted her sleep-tousled curls into place. What would they try next?

CHAPTER THREE

FROM VOLOS, they sailed through the beautiful Pagasitic Gulf and around the Peninsula of Magnesia. Penny had never traveled this way before and under other circumstances would have been delighted with the breathtaking view. To the west were the lush green slopes of Mount Pelion; to the south, the jagged chain of Euboea. And ahead lay the blue-green sea and scatterings of tiny islets in the whitish mist.

Skopelos wasn't a disappointment, either. Not one of the "dry" islands, it was richly forested and pine-scented. Glistening whitewashed houses with blue-tiled roofs clung precariously to the hillside. Fuchsia, carnations and oleander spilled over their balconies in a riot of brilliant color.

Along the quay stood a row of shops, and Steffan, who'd arrived ahead of them, sat waiting at one of the canopy-covered tables outside a small restaurant. He did a comic double take when he saw her and turned his head as if to voice his outrage to some nonexistent companion.

She waved with false enthusiasm and called out to him, relishing the moment. "That look was worth the whole trip," she said to her father with a small giggle.

"I'm glad you think it's funny," Lon grumbled under his breath. "His time is valuable and he's here as a favor to me."

"Do I curtsy or kiss his hand?"

"Neither. You gals wait here. Let me go give him some sort of explanation first."

"Such as telling him I threatened to hold my breath until I turned blue unless you brought me?"

He grinned. "No. Just that you held a gun to my head."

Steffan wore an off-white shirt, its sleeves rolled up to the elbow, and khaki slacks. He was more stern looking than ever with his heavy brows knit in displeasure. He shook his head repeatedly as Lon talked to him, but eventually threw up his hands. Then Lon beckoned to Penny.

To the dismay of her travel-weary body and burning eyes, they were merely moving from one boat to another. Privately chartered, this one was smaller and would rise, fall and leap from wave to wave with the whims of the sea.

For her father's sake and for the sake of a more pleasant outing, she squared herself for another attempt at making friends with Steffan. She wouldn't resort to fawning, but she could apologize for intruding and express enthusiasm for the scenery.

"No picnic basket?" he asked with pseudo-concern as she squeezed past him. "No little cucumber sandwiches with the crusts removed? No iced lemonade?"

"We picked up a bite to eat before we got here," Lon broke in, not giving his daughter a chance to reply. "Shall we be on our way?"

"Maybe the ladies would like to take some snapshots before we go?" Steffan suggested through tight lips. "Did either of you think to bring a camera?"

When she stepped onto the first rung of the ladder, Penny's eyes were level with his, and her prepared apology stuck in her throat. "I've never had any luck with snapshots," she said, making her voice as flat as his. "Beautiful as the scenery may be, something ugly always manages to intrude on the picture."

"You need a lesson," he said, chewing on the remark for a moment before adding, "in photography."

"I doubt that it would do any good."

"Oh, it would. If you had the right teacher." A muscle twitched in his cheek as he grasped her arm more tightly than necessary to help her the rest of the way up.

They waited another fifteen minutes, the women at one end of the boat and the men at the other, plotting in quiet voices, until another man arrived in a rusty pickup. Old Nikko? Not likely. This one was young, powerfully muscled, and carried several large boxes aboard with apparent ease.

At first the water was the stark blue of a splotch from a child's paint set. Then it began to glitter in the sun as if the rippled surface were sprinkled with multihued gems, and Penny recalled the legend of the Sporades, the "scattered islands." When the gods had finished fashioning the world, they had a handful of bright pebbles left. As an afterthought, they soared over the Aegean and let those pebbles fly, creating the islands.

Painfully drowsy, yet too intrigued by the sights to join Wanda in one of the canvas chairs, Penny stood with her arms resting on the rail. All at once a dark spot appeared. The water began to boil and the silvery body of some sea creature appeared and disappeared too quickly to be identified.

Wanda shrieked. "Lord, that was a shark!"

"It was more likely a dolphin," Penny said, leaning closer.

"Oh? Care to take a swim, to prove your point?"

"As a matter of fact, I'd love to."

"If I want a swim, I'll do it in a heated pool. If I want animals, I'll find a zoo." Wanda lit a cigarette and took a puff before lying back with her eyes closed.

Not long afterward, they slid into a twisted channel that seemed barely wide enough to accommodate their craft. It was more shallow here too, and clear, and Penny could discern the dark shapes of sea urchins at the bottom.

Moments later they found themselves in a snug little cove, protected from the force of the capricious island winds—the *melteme*—by a semicircle of high cliffs. A fishing boat, gray and weathered, with *Eleni* painted on its side, sat waiting for them. The muscular young man, who answered to the name of Georgie, secured their boat and lowered a gangplank.

"See you later, gals," Lon sang out, as Wanda and Penny started toward him.

"Aren't we going with you?" Penny asked.

Steffan snorted, but didn't say anything as he hoisted the largest of the boxes onto his shoulder.

"That's Nikko's boat, baby," Penny's father said. "Remember what I told you about him?"

"Yes. He's *another* woman hater."

"He doesn't hate women. He just thinks they don't belong on a boat."

"He has a valid point," Steffan muttered, struggling to manage a second carton by tucking it under his arm.

"I can't say how long we'll be." Lon brushed his lips against the smoothness of Penny's forehead and gave her a hug so quick she hardly felt it. "Be good."

Everything was happening too fast for Penny, not at all the way she'd visualized. She'd expected to trail along with her father and be present at the meeting with Nikko Minotis. Had her father truly come to help out an old friend as he claimed, or were plans being made for another expedition? In either case, she'd hoped to hear the details. How much money was involved, what were the chances of losing it, and most important, was there any danger?

The way things stood, however, there was little she could do without embarrassing her father and reinforcing Steffan's belief that she was an insensitive nag.

"Are we talking minutes or hours?" she asked.

"You elected to take this cruise," Steffan reminded her. "Didn't you bring your embroidery?"

She considered a well-placed kick as he started down the gangplank. The thought of him sputtering and floundering in the water made the impulse almost irresistible.

"There are cold drinks in the cooler." Hastily Lon edged between them, as if he could read her mind. "And Georgie is staying here, in case you need him."

Georgie touched his fingers to his cap and grinned boyishly.

"Cold drinks and Georgie." Wanda yawned. "Take your time. Don't worry about us."

Penny was fairly sure that if she hadn't come along, Wanda would have been allowed to go with the others onto Nikko's boat. Did the woman resent being a baby-sitter? Did she know the real reason for the meeting today? Probably. Lon wouldn't hesitate to tell her. Why should he? Wanda agreed with everything he said and hung on his words as if they were golden. That much was clear from their conversation in the car, during the early-morning drive to Volos. But getting the truth out of her would be impossible, so why waste the effort trying?

Penny decided to forget the negative and concentrate on the positive. The men weren't going anywhere, right now. Obviously everything was still at the talking stage. On the other hand, she was in a breathtakingly beautiful place with nothing to do but enjoy the scenery.

"Would you like to do some exploring?" she asked Wanda, when Lon and the others were out of sight.

"This place is like being in an oven," Wanda complained. "I think I'll lie down."

"You can't mean that. There's so much to see. We passed a wonderful stretch of beach just before we turned in." Penny shielded her eyes and pointed. "Look. There's a path. If we followed it, we could—"

Wanda silenced her with the sweep of one hand. "Surely you jest."

"We didn't come all the way here so Lon and Steffan could say hello to 'old Nikko' and leave. There'll be plenty of time to see what there is to see."

"I repeat. I'm going to lie down until the men are back."

Her own fatigue forgotten with the prospect of a refreshing swim, Penny pulled her green-and-white polka-dot bikini from her overnight bag, along with a matching coverup, and ducked into the cabin to change.

When she emerged, Georgie was waiting, a troubled expression on his face. "I do not think you should go," he told her in schoolbook-perfect but halting English. "Not without asking Mr. Korda."

"I wouldn't ask Mr. Korda the time of day."

"But—"

"Are there dragons out there, Georgie?" she teased.

He looked over one broad shoulder as if he feared there might be. "No, miss. But when darkness comes, it comes quickly."

"Don't worry. I'll be careful."

She'd been right about the path. It took only about a half hour to reach the sandy cove she'd spied, and another twenty seconds for her to discard her coverup and plunge in. The water was wonderful, as she'd known it would be, and she swam until she was too tired to swim anymore.

From where she lay, stretched on the sand to dry, she spotted another path, leading upward to what appeared to be a ruined castle. Scrambling easily over the rocks, she found herself moving between two low walls.

Where the walls had crumbled away, she noticed that the path wasn't an ordinary one. It was a series of ledges gouged out of the rock, forming a circular walkway around the domelike hill. Around and around it went, until there came a break that would allow ascent to another tier. Then another. And another. An effective and exhausting deterrent for any but the most persistent of enemies, the mazelike path required a sharp eye and a sure foot.

Rising to the challenge, she reached the top and crossed a sagging bridge to learn that her castle was only toppled columns and heaped rubble. Though all that remained standing was a tower, three stories high, the sight of it filled her with the sensation of having left her own time and crossed to another, earlier one.

She would have liked to climb the tower's stone steps and view the countryside through one of the narrow windows slit in its side, but she hadn't enough strength left. Besides, she had to think about starting back.

Through the thick-growing pine branches she caught sight of the sky and marveled that the blue deepened as she watched. The cool of evening was in the air. From somewhere came the lonely bittersweet call of a night bird.

"When the darkness comes, it comes quickly," Georgie had said.

He hadn't exaggerated. The fading light made it almost impossible to discover the way down the circular maze. Had there been so many steps before? Had they led downward, only to lurch upward again? When she tried to speed up and bypass one tier, climbing down to the next, she slipped, scraped her leg painfully and almost fell the rest of the way.

At the bottom at last, she looked around for the right pathway down to the cove. There were two. Which was the one that had brought her here? Neither looked familiar.

She chose blindly, imagining her father worrying, and Steffan congratulating himself on being right. Almost at once, she questioned her choice. The slope hadn't been so deep. And it should have been walled. She turned back abruptly, her toe struck a sharp stone and she yelped in pain.

Steadying herself against a boulder, she removed her shoe. But the boulder rolled with her weight, pitched and fell away, crashing many long moments later, far below.

The truth struck her. She had been moving along the edge of a steep cliff. If she hadn't stopped, what might have happened? Would she, too, have gone hurtling into the inky blackness?

With a whimper, she sat down exactly where she was, afraid to walk again in a dark so absolute. She could try to feel about her for a stick and use it to tap her way along. Or should she simply wait until it grew light? They might even come looking for her.

Before she could make a decision, a blood-chilling howl filled the air around her. What kind of beast made such a cry? she wondered, shivering, and rubbing her arms briskly. It sounded almost human. Almost. It must have been huge—and very close.

She held her breath as long as she could, fearing the creature would hear her and seek her out. No. Animals found their prey by scent. Fighting back sobs of desperation, she crouched as low as she could.

The hideous cry struck into the night again. Something was coming toward her.

CHAPTER FOUR

THE GLOW DIDN'T COME from the eyes of some ravenous animal, but from an approaching lantern. It was swung by a bearlike man with black hair like an inverted floor mop, and a beard to match. Whimpering, Penny threw a protective arm across her face.

"Over here," the man bellowed, and two other men came up behind him. One of them was Steffan.

"It's all right, Sparrow," he said gently, scooping her up. "You're safe now."

"I hollered," the bear-man snarled in Greek. "Why didn't you holler back? Fool woman."

"I didn't know what—who—you were," she answered, also in Greek.

"If you know nothing more about these islands than that, you shouldn't be out by yourself. And look at you. All but naked."

"I lost my shoe," she said, nuzzling gratefully against the comforting wall of Steffan's chest, their differences forgotten. "And my robe. It's—I don't know—back there somewhere."

"Would you now have us go to look for it?" the bear-man snorted. "Does it matter nothing that your man has been half-mad with worry for you? Fool woman."

"She's been through enough, Minotis," Steffan said tensely, his voice rumbling deep in his chest, vibrating against her ear. "Let's just get her back and make sure she's all right."

"She would go through much, much more if she were my woman. She would not be running off again soon." Nikko brought his hands to his mouth and, taking a deep breath, emitted the spine-chilling cry Penny had heard earlier. From somewhere far off came another, in answer. "Now, we go," he said. "The others will meet us below."

All the way back he continued his tirade in Greek, obviously not caring that Penny might understand every word.

The need to rescue her had caused a two-hour delay, she soon learned. The delay meant that Steffan would miss his travel connections, along with an important business conference on the mainland in the morning. It also meant that the four of them would have to accept the hospitality of Nikko Minotis for the night.

Her father had been right. Old Nikko didn't hate women—in their place. He had a wife, and her place was in the kitchen. Her name was Eugenie. She was a squarely built woman with somber, close-set eyes and chiseled features. Though she hadn't expected company for dinner, a meal was on the table within half an hour of their arrival.

A stew of huge chunks of wild rabbit and eggplant was the fare, along with beans and mullet, coarse dark bread and thick gravy. Everything was cooked with garlic and far too much olive oil.

Wanda, who'd had the foresight to serve herself, had arranged the food on her plate strategically, to make it look like more. Lon, whose slim build had always belied his ravenous appetite, actually appeared to enjoy the meal. But it was much too heavy for Penny, who'd eaten almost nothing that day. She could only stare at the heaping plate Eugenie Minotis set before her.

"What have you been feeding this one, Mr. Korda?" Nikko asked, gesturing at Penny as he bent low over his dish. "English peas and truffles?"

Eugenie didn't sit at all, but circled those who did. Holding a pitcher and a serving dish, she waited for a chance to replenish the first empty plate or to dash back to the old-fashioned wood stove for more. Nikko and Georgie were quick to indicate with a grunt or a raised hand that they required second—or third—helpings.

To make matters worse, the bear-man's favorite topic of conversation was his joy in hunting. With great enthusiasm he related for them how he had killed, skinned and gutted the very rabbit they were eating.

Penny pressed a hand to her mouth and stood up, letting her chair fall behind her. "I . . . I don't feel well," she explained, heading for the door.

"Come back here, woman," Nikko ordered. "No right-minded person keeps running off so. If I were you, I would see to her, Mr. Korda."

Penny sank onto the porch steps, still holding her mouth, trying to clear her mind of the horrible pictures Nikko had painted. Steffan burst through the screen door seconds later, as if he'd expected to have to give chase.

"Go back inside," she threw at him. "If you don't, you'll never know the proper way to skin a . . . a . . ."

"If you don't mind, I'll stay here." He settled heavily beside her, leaning back on his elbows and stretching his long legs out in front of him.

She studied him suspiciously. "It got to you, too, didn't it?" When he nodded, she went on, "Coward. You make your escape on the pretext of looking after the 'fool' woman."

He grinned and tapped a finger to his forehead. "Guilty as charged."

"What a repulsive man he is. Why didn't you speak up?"

"Why didn't you?"

"What would my objections mean to him? I'm a notch beneath a fox-squirrel. My hide isn't worth as much." As Steffan chuckled, his eyes slid over her, as if he were evaluating her worth, and she felt her face warm. "But you," she added hurriedly. "He actually calls you 'mister.' Your opinion would carry some weight."

"It isn't my place to antagonize the man. This business is important to your father."

"Why is it so important? What's this about?"

His eyes found hers and softened. At that moment he looked as he had the day he'd helped her out of the pear tree all those years ago. He was the Steffan she thought was gone forever. "You'll have to ask him, Penny."

"I knew you'd say that."

Sparrow. He had called her Sparrow when he'd swept her into his arms tonight.

She inhaled deeply, savoring the clean, thyme-scented air, and fell silent beside him. She wouldn't press. Not now. After the rescue, she'd been prepared for his rampage. There had been none. He hadn't even scolded her.

Maybe he didn't despise her, after all. Or maybe it was the full white moon hanging low in the ebony sky. Such a moon was said to touch people and bring about drastic changes in their nature. In Steffan's case, the change had obviously been for the better. He'd been horrid before.

Her nausea was subsiding, but not enough to encourage her to go back inside. Eugenie would probably seat her in front of the heaping plate again. Besides, the rustling, buzzing, chirping sounds of the night were far preferable to the drone of their barbaric host's voice.

"Didn't you hear me holler, woman?" she mimicked, pressing her chin against her chest in an effort to lower her voice to Nikko's pitch.

Steffan laughed. "When you live in these parts, woman, you have to learn the holler of the island folk."

"I do?"

"It's a combination of a shout and a yodel, along with a touch of vibration here." He touched a hand to her throat, to demonstrate.

The casual brush of his fingers—definitely not a caress—caused a stirring deep inside her, and she very nearly forgot herself and responded by smoothing her cheek against his hand, as a cat might when it wants to be stroked.

A scent she'd begun to recognize as only his reached her nostrils, adding to the strangeness of her arousal. Was that arousal part of the full moon's effect, as well? If it was, it had affected him, too. He'd sensed what she was feeling— or perhaps he was feeling the same thing. He allowed his knuckles to skim over her face and down the side of her neck. Neither of them took a breath. She was going to be kissed.

I can't let this happen, she reminded herself. *Not with Steffan. Not until I know the man he has become. Not when the magic of a moonlit sky may only have transformed him temporarily to the man I adored as a child.*

"Let's hear you do it," she said, drawing back.

"Do what?"

"The island holler."

He cleared his throat, opened his mouth, then changed his mind. "I'd better not. If I get it right, Nikko will come charging out that door to find out what it's all about."

"You're right," she said, twisting her mouth comically to one side. "You'd better not. I've seen enough of Nikko for tonight. And I think he's seen enough of me."

Someone inside was playing the bouzouki and singing in a high-pitched, mournful voice. As she and Steffan sat side by side, listening quietly, she tried to study him without his knowledge. But he knew. He was watching her, too, and wondering—as she was.

Perhaps she'd misjudged him. She'd been upset over her father's accident when she arrived, and she realized now that she might have behaved like a shrew without being aware of it.

She owed him an apology in any case. "I'm sorry you've missed your meeting."

"We'll set up another." There it was. One of the expressions she remembered. Briefly it made a dimple appear in his chin. How wonderful to be free to touch a finger to the place. Or, as long as she was dreaming, to press her lips there.

You're mad, girl, she thought, forcing her eyes away. "I couldn't simply sit on that boat and wait, when there was so much to see."

"Forget it."

"What made Nikko think I was your woman?"

"That was your father's idea. It was the only way we could make the man understand why we'd bring you along. Do you mind?"

"I couldn't care less what he thinks. Poor Eugenie. It must be a nightmare living with him."

"You and I started off on the wrong foot, didn't we?" He shifted his weight and turned toward her. For the first time, she felt as if he were actually seeing *her*, not just Lon's intruding daughter, come to smash everything in her path. "You'd already decided I was a despicable monster before you left St. Louis."

"Not at all," she protested, failing to add that she'd reached such a conclusion *after* her arrival. "But I wouldn't say you offered a hand of friendship to me, either."

"Then I'll do it now." He clasped her hand warmly and held it. "Welcome back to Athens, Miss Penelope. I hope you decide to stay."

Did he mean it?

"Why, thank you, Mr. Korda." She lowered her head demurely. "It's marvelous to be here—there. Wherever we are."

"You remind me of your mother," he said suddenly, still holding her hand.

She wrinkled her nose. "I have my father's eyes, his coloring, his hair. Everything. You're the first person to say otherwise."

"The resemblance goes beyond the superficial. It's in your laugh. Your smile. Your voice. The way you move. The texture of your skin."

Was he going to touch her face again? The mere anticipation rekindled the stirring sensation. "I would take that as a compliment, sir," she chided gently, feeling self-conscious about her reaction, "but if memory serves, you don't like my mother."

He settled back on his elbows again and looked at the sky. "When I was a boy, I worshiped her. She was the subject of all my daydreams. She was Helen of Troy. Venus de Milo. Elizabeth Taylor. She was the most beautiful woman I'd ever seen."

Penny couldn't quite believe him. She'd never seen anything but antagonism. "She never knew."

"She knew. I was always underfoot. Picking wildflowers for her, bringing her cold drinks she didn't want, wresting her packages away to carry them for her. I studied her as an artist studies the model he plans to paint. Once she complimented me on a shirt, and I wore it every day for a week. Her favorite poet was Byron. Her favorite song, 'Beautiful Dreamer.'"

Penny looked at him in astonishment. "When I took piano lessons, that was the first piece she wanted me to learn."

"You play?"

"I couldn't get beyond 'Three Blind Mice.' I knew all the notes, but my fingers didn't get the message. What finally happened between you and Mother?"

"My adoration ended abruptly. I was oversensitive to criticism. One day, I'd invited myself along on an outing. You were going—I don't remember—somewhere. I arrived early and heard Connie talking to Lon. She said, 'Can't we sneak off before that boring little wretch gets here? I'm sick to death of looking at him. He has a family of his own. Why must he always intrude on ours?'"

"And you remembered the exact words."

"Yes, I did."

"You were crushed."

"To put it mildly."

"How sad."

"It was a long time ago," he said. But his face was grave. Had he nurtured a grudge all those years?

In these quiet moments, he had allowed Penny a glimpse of the inner man who was Steffan Korda, and she liked that man. With a small, barely perceptible movement of his features, he composed himself. "She did me a favor. I gave up my dreams and threw myself into my studies. I began to learn the business and, finally, to enjoy it."

Penny's mind began to click. The chance had presented itself unexpectedly. "You do understand my concern for my father then?"

"Certainly."

"In that case, will you tell me why we're here? Is he planning some new foolishness?"

The change in his features wasn't as subtle this time. The silence that fell between them was almost frightening, and the joy she'd been feeling sank like a stone. Had she only imagined the dizzying warmth of a moment before?

"You can't let go of it, can you?" he asked.

"How can I?"

He leaned against the porch rail and rose slowly, glaring down at her as if she had somehow betrayed him. "I had hoped we could put aside our differences. Your father is no fool. He's aware of the friction between us, and it disturbs him. Nothing even comes close to matching the feeling a man has for his daughter. He needs her love, her respect and her unquestioning acceptance. Lon and I discussed you at length today, and I promised I'd try."

So that was what tonight had been about. It had only been a pose for her father's sake. "A few ounces of the old charm and a dash of aw-shucks boyishness," she snapped, "and I'm supposed to abandon my principles."

"What have your principles to do with it? What makes you think...? Forget it. I'm going inside."

"Please do. Maybe you can harmonize with Nikko on the next chorus."

Eugenie squeezed past Steffan in the doorway, going out as he went in. "Come along, child," she said in Greek, beckoning to Penny. "The night air is weakening when you are not feeling well."

"I'm fine now."

The men stopped what they were doing to watch as Eugenie closed Penny's hand around a steaming mug of something foul smelling. "Drink this. All of it. I'll make a pallet for you in the back where you won't be bothered by the rowdy behavior of the men. When they've started on their ouzo..." She touched a hand to her forehead at the mention of the powerful Greek liqueur and laughed. "The other woman is already bedded down. She dropped right off to sleep."

Penny sniffed the blackish liquid. It tickled her nose. "What is it?"

"An old recipe of my family's. It cures most everything. Down with it." The woman guided the mug to Penny's mouth and steadied it as she drank. "It's only a pinch of cherry bark, a little pot iron, gunpowder—"

"Gunpowder!" Penny gasped, choking.

Nikko laughed. "She's afraid she will explode through the roof."

Steffan came closer. "Feeling better?" he asked, feigning concern, while amusement played on his lips.

Her stomach did flip-flops of indignation at being subjected to such a brew. More than anything, she longed for a tall glass of clear cool water to chase the foul taste from her mouth. But she wouldn't give Steffan the satisfaction of hearing her ask for it.

"As a matter of fact, I do feel better," she managed, hesitating at first, to be certain she still had a voice. "You say it cures... anything?"

"Anything." Eugenie beamed.

"Then you really should have a dose of it, Steffan," Penny suggested sweetly. "Your stomach has been bothering you all day."

His smile faded, as Eugenie turned her attention to him. "You are not feeling well, Mr. Korda?"

"I'm fine. I never felt better."

"You must not be that way. You men are worse than the children. Wait here. I'll have some stirred up for you before you know it."

As Penny readied herself for bed, she could hear the argument continuing. Eugenie insisting, Steffan protesting. A giddy feeling passed through her and she smiled to herself. Maybe it was the effect of the potion she'd downed. But more likely, it was the certainty that Eugenie would win.

CHAPTER FIVE

THE MESSAGE WAS SCRAWLED on an envelope and fastened to the door of the refrigerator with a happy-face magnet: "You looked so peaceful," it said, "I didn't have the heart to wake you. Had to run and see to a few odds and ends. See you later. Love, Dad."

Penny blew out her cheeks. Run? From the look of him when they'd returned to the Korda villa the night before, he'd hardly been able to walk. His eyes had been mere slits in his parchment-pale face, and she'd decided to forgo the questions.

In the morning, she'd promised herself. They would face each other across the breakfast table. Without Wanda. Then...

But no. He had second-guessed her.

Half a glass of orange juice poured from the carton in the refrigerator, along with a warmed muffin, would serve to still her morning appetite. No need to traipse into the Korda house and disturb the servants or, horror of horrors, risk running into the Lord of the Manor.

No. Penny had plans for the day. She was going home at last.

Humming to herself, she donned her favorite orange-and-white-striped knit top and a divided white linen skirt. Her hair fell obediently into place with only a few strokes of her brush. Was she getting used to it, she mused, studying her mirror image, or was the sheared hairdo not so terrible?

Did Steffan like it? Or was he one of those men who believe only long flowing tresses are feminine?

If she'd arrived with her hair drawn back demurely at the sides, a few wispy curls over each ear, would he have reacted differently? Or if she'd worn a festive shock of all-over curly curls or... No. A sleek, ultrasophisticated twist? Might she have seen a tad more courtesy or consideration?

With a groan, she dropped her hands to her sides and turned away. Why should she give a hoot about Steffan and his preferences? He wouldn't devote a split second to worrying about her.

As she opened the door the heavy scent of roses gave her pause, and on an impulse she plucked a white one and set it in a glass of water in the middle of the table. Then she opened out the envelope that held Lon's note and scribbled one of her own: "See you at home. Be prepared for a feast to end all feasts. Love, Penny."

She'd already guessed how run-down the place would look. Everyone had prepared her with furtive looks and urgent pleas to stay away. The yard would be tangled with weeds and overgrown vines. The inside would be a nightmarish clutter of unwashed dishes, old newspapers and soiled clothing. The rugs would send out clouds of dust with every step.

Could they truly imagine that she cared whether or not her father kept a proper house? It would be a pleasure putting it in order and seeing to needed repairs.

Rather than cut across the tennis courts and down the zigzagging lane to the Haywood backyard, which would have been the shorter route, she chose to circle the front and arrive the same way she'd left, almost ten years before. Homecoming was not a thing to be rushed.

As she drew closer, she moved more slowly, wanting to savor the first sweet moment of return. Then she could only stare. It was home. Yet it wasn't. Once a glistening white, the walls were now a dusty gold. The front window had been made into a sliding glass door. Another room had been added to the north side, and a swimming pool was under construction.

A woman with gray hair tucked into a wide-brimmed straw hat was weeding a zinnia bed. "Are you looking for someone, my dear?"

"I used to...live here," Penny said, feeling as Scrooge must have when confronted with the Ghost of Christmas-Yet-to-Come.

The woman smiled. "Then you can appreciate what we've done. The house was much too small. And it had awkward doors and windows. But where there's enough ground, there's always hope, I say."

Tenants didn't knock down walls or add swimming pools, Penny reminded herself, as the stranger described one after another of the so-called improvements.

"Everything looks very nice," she lied, thinking about the grapevines that used to be where the pool was now. About the missing acacia tree and, under it, the place where they'd buried her beloved dog, Gus.

"The man we bought from said he was a deep-sea diver, or something like that. Is he related to you?"

"He's my father."

"A charming man. Would you like to come inside and see what we've done?"

Never. She'd already seen too much. "No, thank you. I only want..." She allowed her voice to trail off to nothing as she turned away, not wanting the interloper to see the gathering tears.

Through all those starting-over years in St. Louis, she'd clung to the mental picture of the old house. It was a place filled with sunny memories that existed nowhere else. It was her father's anchor, when he came to his senses. It was the sanctuary where she could retreat if the rush and bustle of life threatened to topple her.

Now it not only didn't belong to them, it didn't exist.

Moving one foot automatically ahead of the other, she managed to get out of the woman's sight. She wasn't ready to go back to the Korda house. She wasn't ready to face anyone. Certainly not her father.

The road dipped, climbed, then dipped again. Still she walked. The sun seared her back and neck, but she scarcely noticed.

Over the next hill lay a break in the highway, where an old mule-track led through the pine woods and down to the water. If she followed it, immersing herself in cool tranquil beauty, maybe she could make sense of what had happened. Or was there still a woods? Had it been bulldozed to make way for a towering tourist resort?

The whirr of an approaching car caught her attention, and without looking back, she stepped off the road to allow it to pass. It didn't.

It was silver—low and sleek—and the driver was Steffan, probably sent out by her father to find her. "What's wrong, Sparrow?" he asked, slowing to a stop.

"Don't call me Sparrow. And there's nothing wrong."

"You don't strike me as a woman who cries over nothing."

"I'm not crying."

Groaning in frustration when he didn't drive away, she flung herself away from the car. The matted grass on the slope was thicker than she'd assumed. It sank, her foot slipped and she had to struggle to right herself. Clenching her fists, she allowed a single sob to escape. "Please go away."

"I can't leave you like this." He opened the car door and reached out to her. "Get in. We don't have to talk if you don't want to."

She did as he asked only because she had nowhere to go. He'd soon see what miserable company she could be. If he prided himself on his ability to distract her with his charm, he was going to be disappointed.

Past groves of pomegranate trees, vineyards and terraced plantings of beans and eggplant, the car climbed in the pearly light of midday, with neither of its passengers speaking. The twisting road outlined the cliff edge sharply, wrenching Penny from her introspection. Though Steffan wasn't driving recklessly, she had the sensation that they could spill into the sea at any moment.

As they descended she glimpsed narrow strips of white sand, jade-green water and shadowy blue islands, like so many mirages. Beyond the Bay of Anayssos, they ascended again, and she guessed where they were heading. To Sounion, one of her favorite haunts as a child. How could Steffan possibly know?

There stood the twelve sparkling white Doric columns that remained of the fifth-century B.C. Temple of Poseidon. Built by Pericles so long ago, it stood erect in that high place, welcoming approaching ships and affording the most spectacular view in all Attica.

"Hungry?" Steffan asked, after they had stopped and done a bit of aimless exploring.

Not meaning to, Penny nodded. Accepting his arm, she allowed herself to be led down the rock-strewn path that rambled through carpets of yellow flowers to the beach. There, at one of the little tavernas, they chose a sea-front table and had lunch. It was simple and delicious. *Tiropetes*, triangles of tender pastry filled with feta cheese, along with strawberries in lemon sauce and slices of iced melon.

As they sat watching the waves pound against the rocks, Penny thought of her father and the house again, and shook her head. "It's true that Mother had no part in the house. She didn't have any particular feeling for it. But it's been in my father's family for generations. How could he just give the place up?"

"Lord knows, it wasn't intentional." Steffan beckoned to one of the waiters for coffee refills and waited until they were alone again before continuing. "When he took out the loans to finance a venture at sea some months back, he expected to pay them off easily with whatever he salvaged."

"You're saying he gambled the house away on...on a shipwreck?"

"Does that surprise you?"

"No." She'd seen her father in the throes of excitement over some startling find. Time and time, he'd been hypnotized by the prospect of discovering a king's ransom where some old book or map promised it was. He'd be so adamant about its existence, he would have bet not only his house, but his life. "If he'd only told us he was in financial trouble, Mother and I might have been able to help."

"No one knew, unfortunately. He has more than his share of pride. He's only accepted assistance from me now and then—when I agreed to be full partner in the profits."

"Did you help finance the trip to Peru?" Penny asked the question quickly, as if she could slide it in without making him feel she was snooping.

"Hell, no. He would never have approached me with a crazy deal like that. He knew I'd turn it down."

"Then how...?"

"Search me." Steffan thumped his knuckles on the tabletop. "Your father's made a number of contacts over the years. Some of them less than trustworthy. Business takes me out of the city too much to allow me to know what's going on most of the time. That's why things have been better since Wanda came on the scene."

"Better how?" Penny asked dryly.

"She coaxes him into eating right and keeping fairly regular hours. She's there to build him up when he's feeling down. Sometimes she can make him listen to reason. She can even get him to laugh at himself."

"And other times?"

Steffan smiled crookedly. "More often than not, he convinces her that he's made the find of the century, and she's as enthusiastic about the operation as he is. She goes along with him, and occasionally helps him cover his tracks."

"Exactly. In other words, she humors him."

"At least she lets him know someone's on his side." Steffan's eyes, as dark as the uncreamed coffee he drank, mirrored such gentle concern that Penny couldn't feel angry with him at the implied accusation.

"There are more important considerations."

"Nothing is more important than having someone's complete confidence. Believe me, I know. Lon was there for me when I needed him. I never want to let him down if I can help it."

"When was this?" Penny asked, unable to imagine Steffan—the man he was now, or even the one she knew years ago—needing a boost to his ego.

Steffan tilted his head back and narrowed his eyes. He was silent for a long moment, and when he started to speak, his voice was low, without inflection. "Lon took me through a time in my life that could have broken me. When my father was bitter and hard and saw someone else whenever he looked at me. I was only a boy, trying so hard to please him that my belly was twisted in knots. My fingers were thumbs. I had two left feet. I added two and two and got ten."

"All this has nothing to do with—"

"We went out on those wretched salvage boats and I couldn't do anything right." He didn't look at Penny as he related one tale after another of the times Lon had come to his aid and made him feel there was some good in him. "He was right beside me, reassuring, helping, speaking up for me, making me laugh when I wanted to cry, hauling me out of the water when I was praying it would swallow me up. He was shoulder to shoulder with me, teaching, listening, caring. Being a friend. Being more of a father to me than my own father. I'll never forget that."

Steffan was usually so in control that Penny felt at a loss for words. Neither of them said anything for a very long time. Speckles of sunlight through the fringe of the umbrella that sheltered their table touched his already richly tanned skin with an appealing glow. Falling in love with him when he was like this would have been easy, if she were to give herself half a chance. After all, she had a head start. There was comfort in just being with him, and she was grateful for his quiet strength. But it was more than that. There existed a bond between them. Their affection for Lon.

"Don't you see?" She resolutely ignored the stirrings he'd caused inside her, and thrust aside her coffee cup, leaning forward to seize the moment. "You aren't offering him help. You're offering encouragement."

A frown shadowed his face. "Is there a difference?"

"A big difference. You may gamble along with him. But never more than you can afford to lose."

Steffan glanced toward the next table, distracted. A man and woman in matching souvenir-shop shirts were arguing loudly about whether to go back to the hotel or push on. When he turned his attention to Penny again, his voice was constrained. "You must know there is more at stake here than money."

More than money. How easy it was for people of wealth to voice their contempt for money. Briefly she'd supposed she was reaching him. She wasn't. She'd hoped she might even be able to get some answers about Nikko Minotis and the real reasons behind the urgent trip to the island. Now, she didn't dare to try, or the old argument would begin again.

"Have you ever been forced to mortgage the family home?" she shot back.

"That's not the point."

"It's very much the point."

Kicking off a shoe for emphasis, the man at the next table began to whine that his feet hurt. The woman stood up suddenly and flounced away, shouting that she'd stick to the sight-seeing schedule with or without him.

"Ready to go?" Steffan asked abruptly, as if he felt Penny were somehow responsible for the rude behavior of the pair.

"Yes. Thank you for a lovely day. I've enjoyed it." She meant it, but in another way she didn't, and the words came out tinged with sarcasm.

"Is there somewhere else you'd like to go? Something you'd like to see?" he asked, when he was behind the wheel of the car again. "I have the day free."

"However did you manage it?"

He gestured vaguely with one hand and shrugged.

"Thank you for your offer, but I think not. You've given me enough of your time." There. She'd made her speech gracefully. But she certainly didn't flatter herself that he was sacrificing his day for her. It was obviously his intention to keep her away from her father until she'd accepted the inevitable.

He smoothed his hands along the steering wheel. "If I promise to hold our conversation to a safe topic, will you reconsider? A topic that won't set us sparring again?"

"Do you think there is one?"

He mulled the question over for a moment, then grinned. "How about birds? That always used to work for us."

She touched the back of her hand to her lips to suppress a smile. How foolish all her bird talk must have seemed to him in those days. Yet he'd listened politely and hadn't ever laughed at her. At least, not to her face.

"I believe we've fairly well exhausted that subject."

"Really? You've had a long time to gather new information."

"I've developed other interests."

"Too bad," he said, feigning disappointment.

She'd never known anyone like him. One moment he was tender and considerate, or lighthearted and boyish. The next, he was so impossible she only had to look at him and want to kick him in the shins. Other times—like now—she found herself wondering how it would feel to have those full, wonderfully formed lips crushing hers.

His face was sharply chiseled, making him look older in profile—until he smiled. His was a quick smile, appearing when least expected, throwing her off guard, creating havoc inside her. But it could vanish just as quickly, she knew, and undo all the pleasure it caused.

His blue shirt, sleeves rolled to the elbow as they often were, displayed clearly the strength of his forearms. His well-cut gray slacks weren't snug, but still clung to the lines of his magnificently constructed body. She couldn't help thinking what a perfect model he would be for swimwear. But the thought of Steffan Korda flexing his muscles for the camera was so ludicrous, she had to bite her lip to keep from giggling.

He took the inland route back to Athens, in spite of Penny's protests that she didn't care to play tourist. Ignoring the fact that she was almost a native, he swerved off the main road again and again, and backtracked, pointing out one historical site after another and relating the appropriate myths of each, then insisted they stop and investigate a cave at Koutouki.

Time flew and before she realized it, they were back in Glyfada and Steffan had stopped at a seafood restaurant across from the marina. When Penny argued that they'd just eaten, he argued that he was famished, and proved it by eating everything that was put in front of him and half of what she left on her plate.

Afterward they walked along the water and listened to music from the nearby nightclub.

"I'd better be getting back," she said regretfully. "My father will worry."

Or would he? He probably knew exactly where she was—and who was with her.

At their approach, the high arched gates slid open, then closed soundlessly. Two sleek black dogs leapt to their feet and trotted after them for some distance. By the light of the moon and glimpsed through the graceful linden trees that lined the driveway, the Korda villa with its many balconied windows looked like an ice palace Penny had seen illustrated in one of her old storybooks.

The car moved slowly now. Clearly Steffan had something to say and wasn't sure how to say it.

"Try not to be too hard on your father. The wreck of the *El Capitan*, the one that cost him so dearly, was well documented. I can't say I blame him for going after it."

"His wrecks are always well documented."

"A storm came up and—"

"A storm always comes up. I don't want to hear about it."

Steffan pulled into the garage with a screech of the brakes and turned to face her. "Make up your mind. You said you wanted to know what happened to the house."

"I want my father to tell me about it."

"Meaning you want to rub his nose in it."

Penny clenched her fists. Exit, Steffan the Noble. Enter, Steffan the fire-breathing dragon.

"Meaning there are going to be some changes now that I'm here."

"I advise you to think out your actions carefully. You may do more harm than good if you act impulsively."

"Oh, I've thought things out. Believe me. Unfortunately my father and I are in a position where we have to accept your hospitality, and I am grateful for it. But I can promise you, it won't be for long."

Steffan hit the heel of his hand against the dashboard and groaned in exasperation. "That's just the kind of melodramatic answer I would expect from you."

"Good. I wouldn't want to disappoint you." Letting herself out of the car without waiting for him to play the gallant, she sped toward the guest house, pretending not to hear his explosive protests. Tomorrow morning, early, she would call Sun Dial Sportswear and try to secure a position at once. She and her father would be set up in a place of their own in no time. That would be the first step in freeing him from the Korda sphere of influence.

As she stepped onto the porch, the door swung open. "Oh, kid, you scared me." Wanda slapped a hand to her bosom. "I was just leaving. Lon isn't feeling up to par. He's gone to bed."

"What's wrong?"

"He's been overdoing it, I guess." The woman stood squarely, barring the entrance. "You—you aren't going to wake him, are you?"

"Of course not." Still shaky from her words with Steffan, Penny clamped her teeth down on her lower lip. She knew she owed a debt of gratitude to Wanda for being around to help, but the woman's officious air was so irritating, it made any overtures of friendship difficult.

"How about walking me to my car?" Wanda asked. It was a peculiar invitation, and Penny suspected an ulterior motive.

"Don't you trust me?"

"Maybe I'm afraid of the dark." The woman smiled thinly.

"I thought you might be living in one of the guest cottages, since you're working as Steffan's secretary. He'd want you handy."

"No. I have a cozy little apartment of my own, not far from here." She pointed in the general direction of the city. "How's it going with Steffan?"

"I don't know what you mean." Curious about the turn the conversation was taking, Penny fell into step and the two walked down the path together. "We took a long drive and he helped me through some trying moments."

"You found out about the house then?"

"Did you think I wouldn't?"

"I hope you'll decide not to scold your father. He feels bad enough."

"He isn't the only one."

"The way he saw it, he could either let the chance of a lifetime slip through his fingers, or put the house up to get the money he needed."

"Some choice."

"People find long-lost treasure every day, Penny. I know it sounds unlikely—even impossible. But with Lon's expertise and persistence—"

"You're right," Penny broke in. "It does sound impossible."

"What will you do now?"

"Do? Oh, I'll stay around Athens for a while. Until I can convince Dad to return to St. Louis with me. For a holiday at least."

"You believe you can do that?"

"Why not? He was happy there once. Maybe I can even convince him that a change of scene is a chance for a fresh start." Not to mention the fact the he'd have to abandon any plans involving Nikko Minotis and the island, she said to herself.

"By playing on his sense of guilt?" Wanda slowed to a stop. "By making him feel like an over-the-hill version of a juvenile delinquent?"

"If that's what it takes to save his life."

All traces of friendliness had disappeared from the woman's face. "You have a heap of nerve, I'll say that for you, kid."

"I have to consider what's best for my father. I know him."

"Maybe I know him better than you do."

"Maybe it isn't your concern." Penny was angry now, too. "Dad has an investment in my mother's shop. In a sense, it's his shop, too."

Wanda's laugh was derisive. "Can you see Lon as a shopkeeper?"

"Can you see him as a seventy-five-year-old deep-sea diver?"

"Steffan plans to make a place for him in the business. We've talked about it."

How nice. Wanda and Steffan deciding her father's future for him. "Dad wouldn't accept charity."

"It wouldn't be charity. Lon would be an asset to any company that employed him."

"Then he can easily find a job in St. Louis."

Wanda started walking again. "And he has you in St. Louis. You and your mother." Her voice was bitter.

"He has our full support, yes."

"And you hope it stays that way. Well, don't bank on it."

The woman's confidence was too much for Penny. "You want him to keep on the way he's going at all costs," she accused with a sweep of one hand. "Because if he came to his senses, you might lose him."

"That isn't true."

"Then deny you're in love with him."

Pulling at the edge of the scarf she had knotted around her neck, Wanda stared at the stepping stones in front of her. "I can't," she said quietly.

"Then that's what this conversation is really about, isn't it?" Penny turned away.

"Your mother and father are divorced," the woman called after her. "The sooner you accept that fact, the sooner you'll be able to sort out your own life."

She wouldn't lend credence to Wanda's preposterous suggestion by responding to it. True, she wanted her mother and father to meet and talk things over face to face, as they should have done at the outset. True, she had allowed herself to savor the remote possibility that all these years of failure had left her father ready to jump off the treadmill of broken dreams. To believe that maybe he only needed a nudge in the right direction.

But she wasn't foolish enough to think she could manipulate either of her parents. How had Wanda and Steffan managed to form such a false impression of her?

The lights in the cottage were out. So her father was either asleep or wanted her to think he was. The night was warm and her bedroom would be stuffy. Instead of going inside, she found her way to the swimming pool.

It was in darkness, too, and she wasn't dressed for swimming. But she could sit on the side, dangle her feet in the cool water as she had when she was a child, and try to collect her thoughts.

The house. Gone. El Rancho Contento.

Once Lon had brought home a wooden sign to hang by chains from their gate post. "El Rancho Contento," he'd read aloud, pleased with his find, and ignoring the fact that they were in Greece and the words were Spanish. "A house needs a name."

"It has an address," Constance had scoffed, annoyed that he'd returned late for dinner again. "That should be enough for it."

"How would *you* like a number instead of a name?" he'd thrown back at her, winking at Penny.

"I wouldn't. But *you* might have one some day. Hanging around with no-goods. Listening to their stories. You might be dragged down with them and find yourself behind bars."

It had been one of their everyday exchanges. Good-humored and laced with affection. Teasing, but in earnest.

Constance shouldn't have walked out without a fight. Penny would never forget all those nights after the separation, when she'd heard her mother crying behind her bedroom door. Or the next mornings, when Constance would appear, wearing a brave smile and too much powder, applied to cover tear-swollen eyes.

Sometimes Penny wondered if Lon hadn't loved her enough to agree to a compromise. And sometimes, like now, she wondered if Wanda was right. Was she only holding on to a romantic image, trying to see something that wasn't there?

A clatter to her left caught her attention. Someone was standing on the terrace. Oh, no. It was Steffan. And he was coming toward her. When he was close enough that she could have reached out and touched him, he stopped and looked down at her. A ray of moonlight struck him, illuminating the line of his cheekbones. All action seemed to freeze. They were images on film, stopped in the middle of a melodramatic scene, with neither of them drawing a breath.

"My job offer is still open if you're interested," he said finally.

"I prefer to find something for myself."

"An indepenedent woman." A faint smile touched his lips, then vanished.

"A sensible one. I prefer pleasant working conditions. You and I couldn't get along on a day-to-day basis."

"You came to that conclusion because we blew up at each other once or twice?"

"*We* blew up, did you say?"

She waited for the inevitable jab, but this time it didn't come. "I won't attempt to persuade you to change your mind."

"Thank you for that."

Maybe he would go away and leave her to the healing tranquility of the night. She felt more uncomfortable with him than ever, now that she'd been forced to accept the truth. Despite the hostility between them, there was something even stronger. An undeniable attraction. Yet they didn't even like each other.

"Lon told me that you're part mermaid. If you'd like to swim, I'll turn on the pool lights for you," Steffan offered.

"No. I think I'll go in now."

"Running away?" He uttered the question, if it was a question, almost to himself. But it had been meant for her to hear.

"From you, I suppose."

"From the real world."

She gave her head a small shake. "Aren't you confusing me with my father? He's the one who sees life as something it isn't."

"I don't think so. Lon knows all the pitfalls. He's run into them and knows they're there. He merely has high hopes."

"Isn't that the same thing?"

"Not at all." For a moment, she thought he would kneel beside her. She tensed for it, but he didn't. "When the world isn't all moonlight and roses, when life doesn't trip along as smoothly as it does in the cinema, you stamp your feet, shake your fists and expect your tantrum to change things."

"That's remarkable. And you do it without tea leaves or a crystal ball."

A muscle worked in his jaw. "Your reasons for refusing to work for me, for example. You say we don't get along. What you really mean is that you're used to a different sort of man."

Now it was her turn to mutter under her breath. "You can say that again."

"You're a lovely young woman and you expect men to notice. You expect them to..." He gestured impatiently, searching for the phrase he wanted. "To make passes at you. If they don't, you're confused. You don't know how to handle it."

"Believe what you like," she said in a singsong tone, looking around for her shoes as she stood up.

"If I had kissed your hand or complimented you on the reflection of the sea in your eyes, or the sun in your hair today, we'd be fast friends." He was looking at her hair now with narrowed eyes, as if he might touch it to illustrate his point. One corner of his mouth twitched slightly. Was he unable to resist a smile at his own cleverness?

He was precariously near the pool. A gentle shove would probably topple him into the water. Had anyone ever done such a thing to him?

Her heart pounded with the thought. Oh, how he deserved it. And the moment might never come again.

With a gleeful kind of madness, she made her move, and in her enthusiasm, must have signalled her intentions. Steffan sidestepped deftly, caught her up and whirled her around until he held her dangling over the water.

"You little witch," he said, laughing. "Maybe you'll get your swim after all."

"Go ahead and drop me," she cried, not dignifying his victory with a struggle.

"Don't tempt me."

She weaved off balance as he set her down, and before she could right herself, he'd thrust a hand around her waist to fasten her against him. "If I had taken you in my arms like this," he said, "and kissed you soundly when we walked along the beach, everything would have been fine between us.''

"It's hard to imagine anyone could have such a gigantic ego.'' With every speck of her will, she drove her gaze into his, defying him to see any weakness or wavering.

"It isn't ego. Anyone's kiss could accomplish the same thing, given the proper setting. I'm a man and you're an impressionable, starry-eyed young woman.'' His grip on her tightened.

Had it been anyone but Steffan who held her, she would have known what he planned to do. But even as he brought his mouth down with tantalizing slowness, she couldn't make herself believe he planned to kiss her.

Not until his lips opened over hers, scalding them, did she know, and then it was too late. The effect was paralytic. She no longer felt like a solid, flesh-and-blood being. She was entirely liquid, warm and flowing, and was being transfused into him.

The roughness of his skin—he was in need of a shave now—should have caused discomfort, but didn't. It might have been the first time a man held her in his arms. The first time her lips had been tasted.

She slid her arms around his neck, wanting the moment to last, and as she did, her knit top inched up, giving his fiery fingers access to an inch of exposed skin. They played there, smoothing, stroking, exploring, laying claim to her.

When she was finally able to take an independent breath, it was weak and shivering.

"Do you see what I mean, Penny?'' Steffan muttered, his mouth moving against hers. "Anyone's kiss could accomplish the same thing. Even mine.''

Anyone's kiss. Anyone.

She jerked her head back as if she'd been slapped and stared up at him.

"What I want to make you understand . . .'' he began.

Strangling a sob, she turned from him and ran, stumbling toward the cottage.

"You've forgotten your shoes," he called after her.

But she didn't answer, or return for them.

CHAPTER SIX

ALEX ZEVOS was the man her supervisor in St. Louis had advised her to contact at Sun Dial Sportswear, and so she did. He and Alex had worked together on a project a few years before. They were friends, and he knew Sun Dial was looking for someone special for their advertising department. Mr. Zevos was glad to hear from her and asked her to come in for an interview at once.

"Your work is impressive," he said, poring over the pages in her portfolio. His English was smooth and comfortable with little trace of an accent, probably because he'd lived many years in the States, and his speech was agreeably lacking in advertising lingo. He had unruly black hair, a large mustache to go with it and an expression that said, "I'm going to like you until you prove to me I shouldn't."

Penny liked him, too. Her interview jitters flew with the first handshake. "Those *Post-Dispatch* ads ran for sixteen weeks," she told him as he came to that page.

"You did the artwork?" When she nodded, he made a clicking sound with his tongue. "You've got a style of your own, lady. You'll make a great addition to our team."

He went on to explain that they'd been using in-house advertising for almost two years. It had worked well so far. The pooled artistic resources of employees who considered themselves part of the family, and consequently understood the image they were trying to project, had resulted in imaginative copy. And the company had saved money.

"We're introducing a new line of swimsuits next season. For the over-fifties. Suits with trim lines and showy fabrics. None of these black or beige jobs with flared skirts that cry 'old lady.'"

"There's a tremendous need for attractive suits," Penny agreed. "Even for younger women who don't have bikini figures."

"Exactly."

After taking her on a tour of the factory, Alex explained that the man she'd be replacing wasn't leaving the company for six weeks. Her job wouldn't start until then.

Six weeks. She might have known it was too good to be true. Regretfully she said she wasn't sure she could accept his offer. There were several other possibilities on her list that would offer more immediate employment, if less pleasant and challenging.

His face fell. "Can you give me a definite answer by Friday?"

"I'm afraid it's definite now."

"No, not now. Think about it and give me a call either way. If it's yes, I'll take you to lunch to welcome you aboard. If it's no, I'll take you anyway. On the chance I might change your mind."

For a change her father was still home when she got there. He was rattling dishes in the kitchen; a pot of coffee stood warming on the stove. He sidestepped over to place a kiss on her cheek. "You take yours black?"

"One sugar. I'll get it." She settled into the dining nook with her coffee and waited for him to sit opposite her. "Steffan and I took a drive yesterday."

He nodded. "I know."

"I needed that drive. I've received one shock after another almost from the moment I stepped off the plane. Why didn't you write to Mother and me about the money troubles you were having?"

His nostrils flared and he stared hard at her. "Why the hell couldn't he have let me tell you in my own way? I intend to pay him back. Every damn cent of it. He knows I'm good for it and he sure isn't hurting."

Penny blinked. "You're...you're talking about Steffan?"

"What choice did I have? I couldn't expect Connie to raise you without any help from me. A woman alone. Then there was the financing for the shop she wanted. How could she have swung it, if I hadn't done my part?"

Penny sipped her coffee, without noticing the taste. "You're saying you borrowed the money you sent to Mother and me each month? The money you sent her to get started in business? My college fund? Oh, Daddy, how much do you owe Steffan altogether?"

He raked a nervous hand through his already disheveled hair. "It's between him and me."

"How much?"

"I don't know exactly. But it's all written down, all legal and proper. I insisted on that."

She felt as if she'd just run five miles. Every inch of her throbbed with emotional exhaustion. Her father was mistaken when he said the matter was between him and Steffan. It was her debt, too.

"Steffan didn't tell me anything, Daddy. Not about the money you borrowed from him."

"Then...?"

"When I went to our old house the other day, I met one of the new owners. It was as if my whole past, my childhood—my identity—had been stolen from me."

"I didn't know the old shack meant so much to you, baby. Your ma hated it." He set his cup down so quickly some of his coffee sloshed onto the table and he mopped at it ineffectually with a napkin he ripped from the table dispenser. "I've had more than my share of rotten breaks lately. Things have got to get better."

"They won't get better by themselves." She clasped her hands over his.

Squint lines formed around his eyes. "What do you think I've been doing all these years? Sitting on my duff? Do you have any idea how much money and work goes into a salvage operation?"

"And what good is it?"

"Listen, little girl, I've made a pretty fair living out of what I've been doing. And all the treasure isn't found at the bottom of the ocean. I've made a bundle out of ransacking old houses, searching through ghost towns and battlegrounds. Why, last spring I dug an old whiskey bottle out of a dilapidated outhouse. It brought ninety-seven dollars. You never know." He chuckled at the memory. "Then there was the time Basil Korda and I fished a 1929 Austin out of the drink. It must have gone down straight out of the factory. You'd never guess what one loco collector gave us for it."

"So you make a hundred here and a thousand there. Averaged out, how much would you say you earn in a year—every year?"

He slid his hands away from hers and rose wearily to put his half-full cup in the sink. "Look. I won't get a gold watch for thirty years of faithful service, but there's a place for freethinkers in the world too, Penelope. Life doesn't have to be all cash registers and car payments. It can be cotton candy and rainbows, too. If it couldn't, it'd be a damned intolerable existence."

She took her cup, rinsed it along with her father's, and set them both on the drainer. Following him into the living room, she slipped an arm around his shoulder.

There was a glazed look in his eyes as he held up a thumb and forefinger. "This close. Do you know how many times I've had a fortune only inches away? Sometimes it was lost in a hopeless botch of legal mumbo-jumbo and court battles I couldn't afford to continue. Over boundaries and such. Sometimes it was weather, or ill-placed trust. Sometimes I was just plain robbed—like I was in Peru. But baby, I know as sure as I'm alive, there's a ship resting on the ocean floor somewhere—waiting for me. She went down with a treasure on board that'd take an emperor's breath away. Maybe she's been waiting a couple of hundred years for me to locate her. But she's there, and I don't plan to disappoint her."

"When I was a little girl," Penny said softly, "I wanted to be a famous ballerina."

"Maybe you didn't want it bad enough." The dreamy quality had dropped from his voice and he sat taller. "What you're saying is that your old man never grew up. For your information, cookie, I've been told that before, and I'll tell you the same thing I told the others. I—"

"Knock, knock," Wanda chirped, bursting through the door with a show of breeziness. She wore trim, navy-blue shorts and a blue-and-white polka-dot blouse that bared slim but muscular arms. "It's a glorious day. What are you two doing inside? Anyone for a game of chess on the terrace?"

"You're on." Lon grinned gratefully and loped toward the bedroom. "What'd you do with that blue shirt you ironed this morning? This one's sticking to me. Think I'll change."

"It's hanging on the back of the closet door."

"The cavalry to the rescue?" Penny asked pointedly, more than a little annoyed at the woman's interruption. She'd hoped to ask her father about Nikko Minotis next, to find out if he was involved in plans for another wild-goose chase. She'd had him talking, and he might have been prepared to tell her the truth.

On the other hand, she'd heard nothing about Nikko since their return from Skopelos. Not even whispers. If the project—whatever it was—had fallen through, maybe the less said about it, the better.

"I think I'll change, too," she said, turning away before Wanda could respond to her barb.

The blue shirtdress she'd worn for her interview at Sun Dial was becoming, but it buttoned right up to the neck and was now threatening to suffocate her. Her off-white summer cotton, with a strand of multicolored beads to accent its scoop neck would allow her skin to breathe, and would still be appropriate for what she had to do.

She couldn't take the job Alex Zervos offered, couldn't allow his company to spend time and money training her, even if she were willing to wait six weeks until there was an opening. Not when she planned to leave the country as soon as she could convince her father to accompany her—for a short visit, anyway. He hadn't been in the States for almost twenty years. Seeing old friends and old places again might make him realize that a different kind of life was not only possible, but desirable.

So she'd take Steffan up on his magnanimous offer and shock him silly by being the most efficient secretary he'd ever had. There would be a stipulation, of course—that a large chunk of her salary be held back in partial payment of what he'd spent on her education. Besides, here was her chance to show him how little their encounter at the pool had affected her. He'd just caught her at a weak moment. If she remained prim and unflustered in the face of whatever he threw at her, he would begin to believe he'd imagined the whole humiliating incident.

Following the maid's directions, she found his study and tapped lightly on the door.

"Come in."

With the blinds closed against the afternoon sun, the room was oppressive, all dark paneling and oxblood leather upholstery. How sharply it contrasted with the airiness of the rest of the house—the pale walls and carpets, with throw pillows, flowers and carefully selected art objects adding accents of turquoise and apricot.

Steffan sat sorting through a stack of papers, looking unapproachable in reading glasses. He glanced at her without reaction, then went back to his reading. After scribbling something on one page, then another, he removed his glasses, put them into his pocket and pressed his fingers to the bridge of his nose.

"You've changed your mind about the job, I assume. Can you start now?"

Nothing like being predictable. "By now, you mean—"

"At once."

"Well . . . yes." She hadn't envisioned being hired so quickly, and without having to recite her qualifications. But then, he knew about her education, didn't he? He'd financed it.

"Wanda will work beside you for the first week," he said, "and help you begin your routine. If there's anything you don't understand, ask her. Although the work isn't demanding, it's precise. I insist on having things done the way I want them done."

Penny considered a suitable retort, but rejected it. Now that he was her employer, she would treat him with respect, despite their differences.

"Sit down, please." He nodded toward the chair beside his desk, and when she'd settled, handed her some pamphlets describing the history and operation of the Korda Inns.

He was wearing a white dress-shirt, but had discarded his tie. Oddly enough, dark as he was, the hair at his wrists and the opening of his collar was almost golden. His watch was plain gold with an old-fashioned face and a brown leather band. His were capable hands, not small, not huge, but squarish with blunt fingertips. He wore no jewelry other than the watch. Not even a ring.

Enough inventory-taking, she scolded herself. There was no future in feeding leftover schoolgirl infatuations. The past was dead.

She narrowed her eyes ever so slightly, trying to see some resemblance to his father. Basil Korda would have been the subject of no sensible woman's dreams. Grossly overweight, he'd had bloated features, a coarse laugh and a greedy mouth. Given a few years—who could say?—Steffan might look exactly the same.

Except she knew he wouldn't. Steffan wasn't Basil. She remembered the way Steffan's arms had tightened around her. And the taste of his kiss that lingered with her even now.

"My father was the one who had this library furnished," he was saying. "Now and then I'm tempted to have it done over, but . . ."

He didn't finish the sentence; it wasn't necessary. Penny could feel the older Korda's presence, and not only because of the portrait that glared down at them from over the file cabinets. Changing anything would be like evicting a ghost. But then, in this case, would that be so bad?

"It certainly is a no-nonsense room," she said, feeling a need to make some comment.

Steffan got up to return a thick leather-bound volume to its slot in the bookcase. "I'd like you to meet me at my downtown hotel at eight o'clock."

"Tonight?"

"Tonight. Be dressed for dinner and dancing."

Was this a roundabout way of asking her for a date? The grandfather clock in the corner was ticking so loudly it might have been mimicking her heartbeats. Was it possible that, despite his self-confidence, Steffan found it difficult to come right out and ask her? He had to be brisk and businesslike? Had he also found it difficult to forget how they'd felt in each other's arms? The way she had?

He rifled through the desk drawer, brought out a business card and thrust it at her. "Go to this shop, find a dress that suits you and charge it to me. I realize there won't be time for a proper fitting, but that can't be helped."

She swallowed hard, confused by the fuss he was making. "Steffan, I have something to wear."

"You'd better hurry." He glanced at his watch and groaned, apparently not hearing her. "You may want to have your hair done as well. But I don't suppose you have the proper license for driving in Athens."

"As a matter of fact, I do. Earlier this year, I'd planned to—"

"Good girl," he cut in, digging through his desk again. "The tan Saab is at your disposal. It's in the garage."

"This is happening so fast."

"I know, and I'm sorry. The whole thing came up unexpectedly. Your decision to take the job couldn't have come at a more opportune time." He brushed her hand as he dropped a set of car keys into it, and all sensation rushed to the spot. "I'm entertaining a client from Los Angeles tonight. He and his wife want to see Athens-after-dark, and I need you to round out the foursome."

She drew her hand away and made a fist around the keys. "I see."

"An attractive woman on a man's arm is the perfect window dressing." He smiled briefly. "To make a business deal more palatable."

He only wanted her to "round out a foursome" and had the gall to tell her so? How dare he assume that a salary would put her at his disposal night and day? Where were all the simpering female companions she'd seen with him in the old days? Why didn't he treat one of them to a night on the town?

No. It made sense. If he were to take one of them, he'd have to worry about showing her a good time. Penny was on the payroll. He could ignore her feelings and concentrate on business.

Window dressing, was she? Back at the cottage, muttering to herself, she went to the refrigerator, unscrewed the cap of a giant soft-drink bottle and poured some of the contents into an ice-filled glass.

"I'll be your dinner companion tonight, Mr. Korda," she told her absent employer, with a mock toast. "But my hair will stay exactly as it is. There isn't anything very glamorous that can be done with it anyhow. As for my dress, you'll darn well accept me in the one I bought on sale. Just thank your lucky stars I don't turn up in blue jeans and sneakers.''

CHAPTER SEVEN

PENNY SWALLOWED her stage fright as she rode the hotel elevator up from the parking area to the lobby. Steffan was her employer, not her master, and a temporary one at that. It wasn't necessary for him to approve of her appearance.

The new shampoo she'd tired had left her hair looking like polished gold against the smoothness of her summer tan, and the shimmering turquoise of her shantung dress gave her eyes a jewellike sparkle. She loved the color now as much as she had when she'd bought it, and the full swing of the skirt made it perfect for dancing. She wasn't entirely comfortable with the bodice, though. Its shirring allowed for the fullness of her breasts and still tapered cleanly to emphasize her narrow waist. But was it too bare, with only a narrow strap at each shoulder?

She had studied the effect with and without the necklace several times, before deciding to leave the neckline unadorned. Now she wondered.

Steffan was distractingly handsome in his dark suit. He favored her with a dazzling smile, and for a moment, she thought he might go as far as to kiss her hand. It was easy for him to play the part of devoted escort, she decided, matching him tooth for tooth. He had only to visualize the mountain of money he would realize from the deal he hoped to close that night.

The client, Franklin Lacey, had sloping shoulders, a slow drawl, and a comical way of rolling his eyes. His wife, Verna, was half a head taller than her husband, large-boned and beautifully proportioned in a black, skintight evening dress. She would have been stunning if she hadn't been wearing a towering platinum wig that drew stares.

Penny didn't need extrasensory perception to see that what the woman felt was instant hate. Verna Lacey resented her, probably as she resented most members of her own sex.

After the introductions they were taken on an impressive tour of the high-rise Korda Inn. Then it was a delicious dinner, beginning with a staggering array of appetizers and ending with a flaming dessert, in the top-floor dining room, which revolved to allow a superlative view of the city.

At Verna's request, they went to one of the popular tavernas on the Plaka, where they drank retsina and listened to santuri music. One after another, the men got up and did the *zeinbekkos* and the *khasapikos*. Franklin would have joined in, too, if his wife hadn't held him in his chair.

She'd had enough, she said. She despised the music and the food and the old fools who got up to whirl around the room by themselves. Though Steffan tried to explain the state of exuberance that caused the dancers to forget their surroundings and dance for sheer joy, she concluded loudly that they all had "a few screws loose."

She wanted a disco nightclub, where they could dance like "civilized" people. When they found one that suited her, Franklin declined, and Steffan became her unwilling partner. To Penny's difficult-to-disguise amusement, Verna had him doing the most acrobatic sort of dancing imaginable, and by the fourth or fifth number, he began to wilt under the strain. Still he managed what passed for a smile and even a laugh when it was called for.

Penny would have enjoyed his discomfort more if she hadn't had troubles of her own. Franklin might have been slow talking, but he wasn't slow moving. He'd pretend to call attention to something across the room and "accidently" brush a hand across her breast. Or he'd laugh heartily and slap her on the knee in his enthusiasm. When he lured her onto the terrace "for some air," and wrestled for a kiss instead, she had to put him in his place. Fortunately he didn't seem offended.

"St. Looey woman," he crooned against her ear, as they went back to the table, where his wife and Steffan were waiting after their most recent performance on the dance floor.

"We were getting some—" Franklin began.

"I know damn well what you were getting!" Verna snapped.

At last the band played a slow number and Steffan asked Penny to dance, probably because he felt it was expected of him. But she didn't mind. Not only did she feel sorry for him, she welcomed a respite from Franklin.

"Is it going badly?" she asked, when they were on the floor together.

"What do you think? I haven't had a word with Lacey all evening, and they're flying back to Los Angeles in the morning."

"Oh, I'm sorry."

"What is it you two are finding to talk about?" The groove between his eyebrows deepened. "Maybe if you didn't try so hard I could make some progress."

"I'm only being friendly."

"Try being friendly with his wife. Can't you see you're antagonizing her? And that dress you're wearing is so damned...provocative."

"What's wrong with my dress?" she demanded angrily. The reasons for his accusation were so obvious. He was no better than a small boy making excuses for having lost at a game of marbles.

"It's lovely. What there is of it."

"So. My secret is out," she threw at him. "I have shoulders."

"Yes, you have." He let his eyes glide over them. "Do you find it necessary to flirt with every man you meet?"

"Flirt?" She tilted her head back to look fully into his face. "Maybe if you weren't out on the dance floor every minute, behaving like a character in *Saturday Night Fever*, you might have been able to accomplish what you set out to accomplish."

He glared at her with new ferocity, and she tried to glare back, but couldn't. The memory of Steffan on the dance floor, cavorting like an overzealous teenager, was too fresh in her mind, along with the panicky look he tried to contain each time Verna leapt up, reached for him and said, "Shall we go for this one, Stevie?"

When Steffan tightened his hold on Penny, jolting her closer, she thought he would shake her, or at the very least, launch a fresh verbal attack. He didn't. He pressed his lips tightly together, but only in an attempt to suppress his own laughter. When he couldn't, he executed several turns taking them to the opposite side of the floor—where the Laceys couldn't see them and wonder what they found so humorous. For several minutes, he and Penny had only to look at each other to trigger a new fit of laughing, until tears filled her eyes and she felt weak with it.

"This is a nightmare," Steffan said finally.

"What are you going to do?"

"I haven't given up yet. Invite Verna to the powder room. Keep her there as long as you can. Admire her hairdo."

"Nobody in their right mind would admire her hairdo."

"Tell her what a sensational dancer she is. Ask her to show you a step. Ask her advice. Anything. Use your imagination."

"The woman despises me. She's rude and insulting."

"I don't give a damn if she's Lucretia Borgia. Do your job."

It was nearly four o'clock in the morning when they said their good-nights and left the Laceys at the hotel. Penny hadn't been able to lure Verna away from the table, and the outing had come to a disastrous conclusion, with Verna accusing Franklin of pawing Penny and Franklin snatching Verna's wig and throwing it out the car window.

Philosophical about their failure, however, Steffan was in a good mood as he drove home, explaining to Penny why he'd hoped to convince Lacey to sell his property. Acquiring it would have allowed needed expansion of the Korda Inn in Los Angeles.

"These things happen," he said with a shrug, then went on to recount one of the more hilarious highlights of the Verna-Franklin match that evening. Penny reminded him of another, and from the way they were laughing as they pulled into the garage at the Korda villa, anyone would have thought the evening had been a smashing success.

"Sleep as long as you like," he told Penny. "I won't expect you in the office until afternoon."

"I'm fine. I don't even feel tired."

"Ah, youth," he said with a raised eyebrow. "Just the same, you may feel differently once your head hits the pillow."

"I don't think so." She studied him out of the corner of her eye, wondering if this was the right moment to broach an uncomfortable subject.

They were on Korda property and within shouting distance of the Korda house. Yet here and now, within the confines of the car, she didn't feel intimidated by him. They were a man and a woman together, like any other man and woman who'd shared an evening.

"There's something I have to talk to you about before we go in," she said quickly, afraid she might change her mind.

He squinted at his watch, but made no reference to the late hour. "Go ahead."

"It's about my salary."

He closed his eyes and opened them wide, affecting an expression of incredulity. "You want to talk salary at four o'clock in the morning? It will be generous enough, I assure you."

"It isn't the amount that concerns me."

"You're thinking about a retirement fund, sick leave, dental plan?" He drummed his fingers on the steering wheel.

"No." She considered each word carefully before she uttered it. "I want to make arrangements to pay you back as soon as possible for the money you spent on me."

"What are you talking about?"

"The money you gave my father for my education."

"Business between Lon and me has nothing to do with you." There was an edge to his voice, as his boredom moved toward anger.

"I don't see it that way."

"I don't give a damn how you see it." He pushed away from the wheel, straightening his arms in front of him in an effort to check his temper. "My debt to your father far outweighs his debt to me. I'm not going to sit here and quibble over a few dollars. Especially not with you. As far as I'm concerned, he could have this whole bloody house and everything in it."

"I understand," Penny said, determined to say the words she had rehearsed, whatever the consequences. "But please understand how I feel, too. The debt we're talking about now is mine, and I feel obligated to pay it. All I'm asking is that you hold back half of my salary. It'll be painless that way, and it'll be a start, at least, at getting things squared away between us."

"I don't hire slave labor."

"And I don't accept charity."

"You'll earn every cent you're paid."

"Will I? You evidently weren't satisfied with my performance tonight," she reminded him.

"Tonight wasn't your fault. May we go in now?"

"I'd like to settle this first." She'd come this far. She'd carry it the rest of the way.

"You're behaving like a headstrong child."

"Take a good look at me, Steffan. I'm not a child."

"Used to raising hell to get your way, aren't you?"

"Aren't you?"

He dismissed her question with a sweeping gesture. "That's different."

"Because you're a man? Or because you make more money in a week than I'll ever see in a lifetime?"

"Money." He emphasized the "m" sound comically, and flexed one hand, opening and closing the fingers several times, as if he needed to see if they still worked properly. Then, without looking away from Penny's face, he loosened his tie. "I might as well get comfortable."

A warning sounded inside her brain as he edged toward her and allowed his arm to slide around the back of the seat, brushing her shoulders. It was a casual movement, not one that seemed studied. A movement made in the interests of relaxation. But why had the air suddenly become thick and still? Why did she have trouble taking a proper breath? They weren't isolated from the rest of the world, so why should she feel they were?

She wouldn't press him further. He hadn't agreed with her, but he was a moderately reasonable man. When he mulled over her remarks, he would reach a sensible conclusion.

"I suppose you're right," she told him hesitantly. "About the hour, I mean. It's late and there isn't much more to say."

"You wanted to talk. I'm ready to listen." Absently he fingered one of the strings that held her dress in place. "It's easy to see why Lacey was smitten with you. You're a vision in that dress."

Was the comment another, more subtle criticism of what she'd chosen to wear? "Maybe I should have worn a tent," she threw at him, hoping to get herself back on solid ground.

"It wouldn't have helped." Inhaling deeply, he brushed his lips against her hair, then burrowed through the curls, slightly tousled now, to find her earlobe, numbing her from toes to eyebrows.

"Don't." She drew back, needing to keep space between them. "Why, whenever we have a difference of opinion, do you end up threatening me?"

He laughed gently at her overreaction and raked her toward him again, renewing his assault on the same ear. "How am I doing that, Sparrow? How am I threatening you?"

It hadn't been what she'd meant to say. If there was a threat present, it was only in her reaction to his nearness and to the knowledge that almost anything he said or did at this crucial moment would crumble her remaining defenses.

He, on the other hand, was making light of her concerns. He was switching their employer-employee relationship to man-woman, letting her know that he thought she was blowing trivialities up to gargantuan proportions.

"Don't," she gasped again, as the hand that had been smoothing her shoulder began to caress her face, urging it toward his.

"Don't...what?" he murmured, as his breath, moist and warm, tantalizing and irresistible, mingled with hers.

"If you kiss me, don't pretend you're doing it to silence me."

"I won't."

"And don't pretend you're doing it to prove a point."

"I'm not trying to prove anything," he assured her, using the movement of his lips to coax hers apart, allowing him to lay claim to them.

With the scalding pressure of his mouth came the exquisite pleasure she'd felt when he had kissed her before. The same, but not the same. There was more, so much more. The slow-burning fuse, ignited when their lips first touched, had done its work well. The explosion was stunning. An as yet untapped vein of passion opened within her, and her muscles sagged with it.

Her thoughts, dizzying and fragmented, were made up of unanswerable questions. What would she have done if he'd listened to her when she protested his kiss? What torment would she have experienced if he'd bowed to her wishes and moved away? If they had gone into their separate houses and the night had ended without this miraculous sharing?

Each of Steffan's kisses, one feathery and teasing, the next hungry and demanding, another testing and tentative, was more consuming than the one before. She said his name carefully, wanting to experience the sound of it, wanting the full spectrum of its meaning to still the war she'd waged against him, and so against herself. Tomorrow Steffan Korda would be the same man he'd been yesterday and today. Yet he would be entirely different.

Reality was so much better than fantasy, she marveled, allowing her hands to play freely at the back of his neck, luxuriating in this new privilege of memorizing with her fingers the unique pattern of his crisply waved black hair, and at the same time, making him a prisoner with her own kiss.

"Sparrow," he whispered against her mouth, and his arms enveloped her with fierce possession. His lips slid lower, to the vulnerable hollow of her throat, and lingered there.

He was not indulging in pretense now, as she at first had supposed. He wasn't using her to sharpen his already expert powers of seduction. No, he was filled with wonder, as she was, and the knowledge brought her inexplicable joy.

"It'll be light soon," he said so softly she hardly heard him.

"Mmmm." Had he drawn back ever so slightly?

"We'd better go in." The shuddering breath that resulted from his monumental efforts at self-control, spiraled through her, too, as he placed a final kiss on her shoulder and sat up.

"I'm not tired," Penny said.

"I am. And I have to get up in a couple of hours to drive the Laceys to the airport."

She smiled at him lazily. "Do you want me to come with you?"

Penny's unlikely suggestion, considering Verna's undisguised loathing of her, drew a fleeting, but pulse-stirring smile from him. "Uh . . . no thanks. You'd better get some rest."

Rest, perhaps. But not sleep. She had too much dreaming to do for that. The best kind. The wide-awake kind with a firm foundation in reality and its delicious possibilities.

"What happened to the goldfish?" she asked as they passed a rock-bordered pool that had surely once been wriggling with water-life.

"My father had the pool drained long ago."

"Why?"

At first she thought he hadn't heard her. "It belonged to my mother," he finally said, as if the words were self-explanatory.

Penny grasped his hand and held it while they walked. What a bewildering, frustrating, but completely beautiful night this had been. And what an overbearing, thoroughly maddening, tender and beautiful man Steffan Korda was.

He was walking her to her door as he might have if they were teenagers returning from a special date. Would he kiss her good-night on the porch? If not, she would kiss him. She needed the feel of his lips on hers once more, or she would never be able to close her eyes that night.

As the path curved to carry them under a thickly vined trellis, she was overcome by the impulse to stop there. The persistent chirp of the crickets, the warm smell of blossoms, somehow sweeter at night, and the poignant cry of a night bird—all of that, and Steffan's presence, made her want to capture the moment, to hold it in her memory for all time. In years to come, she would close her eyes and remember. This was how it was. This was how it felt.

Taking three steps to Steffan's one, she moved in front of him and turned, creating a small collision. And a mind-shattering opportunity.

He didn't laugh or take her in his arms, though. He only reached out to steady her. His eyes were shadowed. "I hope you can forgive me for the way I've behaved," he said, with the stiff politeness of someone who was begging her pardon for jostling her in a crowd.

She almost giggled, but didn't. Something told her he wasn't joking. "What is there to forgive?" Was he talking about their first encounter and the way it ended? Or about the second? Did he mean both of them?

He moved a hand slowly across his forehead. "You're Lon's daughter. I . . . I shouldn't have taken advantage of you."

"I'm not sure who took advantage of whom."

"I'm being serious."

"So am I." The cry of the bird came again, but this time it sounded more raucous than melodious. "I'm not just Lon's daughter, I'm *me* An individual. A person." *A person who is beginning to care deeply for you*, she wanted to say, but didn't.

"You're Lon's daughter first. I owe him too much to allow this to happen."

"You didn't allow anything to happen. I'm not Alice in Wonderland. I know what I'm doing."

"Do you?"

Was he saying what she thought he was saying? If he felt their relationship was a real and lasting one, he wouldn't be worrying about Lon. He must know her father would have led the cheering section. No. He meant that what they felt for each other was mere fascination, soon to die a natural death.

Anger began churning inside her, mixing with the hurt to make it more intense. "You're saying that what happened between us tonight was born out of sheer lust. Any female with the standard equipment would have had the same effect on you. If it hadn't been me in your arms, it could have been anyone."

It could have been anyone. Wasn't that exactly what he'd said to her the last time they'd kissed? Anyone.

"Don't put words in my mouth."

"I'm only paraphrasing."

"I don't need an interpreter."

"No, you don't. I suppose I should feel lucky that you're such a gentleman. What we had tonight was just a chemistry lesson."

"Sparrow." He reached for her hand, but she yanked it vehemently away.

"When I was in high school," she said, "the course with the lowest enrollment was 'advanced science.' All the kids thought it was boring. Maybe if the teacher had presented the concepts your way, he would have had a full house."

She turned her back to him, wanting to throw her hands over her face in despair. Except it would only confirm what he probably already believed. That she'd assumed too much. That she'd twisted a biological impulse and the resulting flirtation into something more.

"You're very special." He rested his hands lightly on her shoulders. "Everything about you stirred me from the first day—the first moment—you walked onto the terrace. I'd never seen lips I wanted so badly to kiss. Your eyes, your voice..."

"And you naturally analyze your reactions every time you take a woman in your arms."

"I wish I could. It would have saved me a lot of grief."

"Poor baby. I'll save you, if you can't save yourself." Clenching her fists, she wrenched herself free and began walking. "Find yourself another secretary."

"Penny—"

"No! Wait." She took only a few steps before whirling around, her eyes blazing. "I won't quit. That's what you'd like me to do, isn't it? So you can wash your hands of me and tell my father you tried? Forget it. You'll have to fire me, and it won't be easy, because I'm capable and efficient." She moved backward, holding one hand in front of her to ward off his advance.

"Will you stop the hysterics for a moment and listen to me?" he tried.

"So I turn you on, do I? Good. Take lots of cold showers. Because if you even look as though you might touch me, I'll leave a handprint on your smug arrogant face that'll be black and blue for a week."

Inside the cottage, she groped her way through the semi-darkness to the bathroom.

"That you, honey?" Lon called in a sleep-filled voice. "Have a good time?"

"Oh, yes," she said through clenched teeth. "Wonderful."

CHAPTER EIGHT

STEFFAN HAD GONE by the time Penny arrived in the office at nine o'clock sharp, postponing what would likely have been an uncomfortable few minutes.

Wanda was almost hidden by a stack of files on her desk. Two pencils were stuck crossways through the mane of her piled-high hair. She sighed and looked around at the clutter apologetically. "I'm supposed to show you the working of things. But now I have a problem. A misplaced report, somewhere in all this."

Penny knew the feeling. "Can I help?"

The woman gestured toward the open door that led to an inner office. "Steffan has dictated some letters for you to do. They're on the tape machine on his desk. Just flip the switch and follow instructions."

Steffan's voice was crisp and authoritative. It was probably a deliberate attempt on his part to sound stuffy, otherwise his incredibly sexy tones might have thrilled her to the point of distraction. She was to type the letters he dictated, four of them. Then she'd be free for the rest of the day to relax, swim and make up for her "late night," unless something important came up.

After satisfying the child within her by favoring the dictaphone with a grimace, complete with stuck-out tongue, she went to work and was finished quickly.

"Now what can I do?" she asked Wanda, who had removed the contents of two drawers and had the folders separated into innumerable stacks on the floor.

"Just answer the phone, if you will. Say Mr. Korda isn't expected until after three and take messages. I don't think there'll be many calls, though. Everyone knows about the meeting this morning."

She was right. The phone didn't ring. Penny waited patiently, but doing nothing had always been difficult for her. After a while she picked up a pencil and began to doodle. Swimsuits. Words and catch phrases. An idea struck her for the new line of sportswear Alex Zevos had told her about, and her enthusiasm grew. Taking out a clean sheet of typing paper, she began to sketch. Another idea. Another sheet of paper, another sketch.

"Eureka!" Wanda squealed from the outer office. "I found it." Seconds later the typewriter keys were clattering.

Penny studied her drawings. Though they were only rough ideas, they were really quite good. Her favorite was a series of three cartoon-style sketches. In the first, a sad-looking woman was wearing a bathing suit that looked more like a tent. "Forget Safe," the caption read. In the second, the same woman wore a droopy black suit whose skirt reached her knees. "Forget Sensible," it said. The third picture showed the same woman smiling as she hurled aside the unattractive garments. The suit she wore now was bright and becoming. "Think Sensational," bold letters advised. "Think of *you* in a Sun Dial Swimsuit."

Another drawing showed a woman hiding behind a tree, afraid to join the beach crowd. "Nobody's perfect," Penny had swirled underneath. "So let Sun Dial find the right shape for the shape you're in."

The comically miserable expression on the woman's face made her smile. She held the sketch at arm's length and cocked her head to one side, trying to get a fresh perspective on it and wishing she could share what she'd done with Alex. It would be fun to see what he thought.

Alex. She picked up the telephone, remembering that she'd promised to let him know whether or not she'd take his job offer. There was little point in making him wait for her answer, especially when she had time on her hands.

As she suspected, he wasn't happy about her decision. "We agreed to talk about it on Friday," he protested.

"Another day or two wouldn't have made a difference."

"And what about our lunch?"

"That was only if I took the job."

"It was also if you didn't, remember? Hey, how often do I run into somebody I can swap inside stories with about the gang in St. Louis?"

"I don't know." Penny squinted sideways at one of her sketches, studying it as though through Alex's eyes.

Persuasion was an advertising man's forte, and her indecision allowed him to bring his talent into full play. Before she'd hung up, she'd agreed to meet him for lunch. Why not? As her new boss said on his tape, she had the rest of the day off.

"I've already put in a full day's work," Wanda said, bursting in to thrust something into Steffan's file cabinet. "Think I'll leave now and catch some sun. How about joining me?"

"Maybe another time," Penny said absently, setting her drawings side by side on the desk in front of them. Which was best?

Wanda looked over. "I didn't know you were an artist."

"I'm not . . . exactly. I'm in advertising. That is, I was."

"These are very good . . . I think. But then, what do I know?" The woman stuck her sunglasses on the end of her nose, adjusted the strap of her handbag and started out the door. "Oh, don't forget to click on the answering machine when you leave. Okay?"

Penny nodded. She picked up a pencil, using its eraser to clean up some smudges, and its business end to add a bit more detail here and there. True, it was only an idea, but she wanted to present it as attractively as possible. There was always a chance she could make an arrangement with Alex to do some free-lance work for Sun Dial. That would provide an opportunity to make extra money and pay Steffan what she owed him all the sooner.

The phone at her elbow jangled.

It was a woman from the downtown-Athens Korda Inn. She wanted to speak with Miss Rice. When Penny told her Wanda had gone for the day she groaned.

"Will you look in the center drawer of Steffan's desk? There should be a blue folder marked 'Environmental Impact Report.'"

"There is," Penny assured her, seconds later.

"Thank heavens. Can you slip it into a briefcase and bring it to the hotel at once? Steffan will be waiting in the lobby for you. The conference can't progress much further without it."

When Penny brought the car around Wanda was sitting on the cottage steps. She'd changed into a brief lime-green swimsuit and was rubbing coconut oil on her shoulders. "You missed Lon by seconds," she said amiably.

Penny didn't bother asking where he'd gone. She opened the Saab's door, rolled down the windows to give the car a chance to air, and set the briefcase with Steffan's Environmental Impact Report on the passenger seat. Regretfully she looked at the manila envelope that held her Sun Dial sketches, and sighed.

"What's wrong?" Wanda wanted to know.

"Nothing really. I was supposed to meet someone for lunch."

"And now you can't?" She stood up and came over to the car.

"After you left I got a call from the hotel. Steffan wants me to bring him this report." Penny thunked her fingers against the briefcase.

"Could I do it for you?"

"Dressed like that?"

"I can change." Wanda took a step toward the house.

"There isn't time. A meeting's waiting for it. But thanks. I'll just have to cancel my lunch date."

"Never turn down a free meal, kid. Where are you supposed to eat?"

"At a place called Bretannia's."

"Ah, yes. When?"

"In forty minutes."

"You can do both with time to spare."

"You think so?"

"Easily." The woman smiled. "Go. And enjoy."

Inside the cottage, Penny splashed water on her face, brushed her hair furiously to tame it and lend it a shine, then powdered her nose and repaired her lip gloss. After considering her slim white skirt and dark-gold cotton shirt, she decided the outfit would do—with the addition of her white blazer to add a businesslike touch. There wasn't time for anything more. She wouldn't wear the blazer, though, until she got to the hotel parking lot. It was too warm.

There was no need to search for Steffan. He was in the lobby as the woman who called had said he would be, pacing. He was playing the starch-collared, cool-browed executive to the hilt. Only the subtle scent of his shaving lotion identified him as the man who'd rocked her world off its foundations the night before.

She needn't have worried over how she looked or how she should greet him after their previous intimacy. He wouldn't have raised an eyebrow if she were stark naked and held a rose in her teeth. All he saw was the briefcase.

"Good girl," he said, with a flash of even white teeth that was meant to serve as a smile. "Now we can get rolling."

"Good girl," she repeated to herself as he turned on his heel and was gone. It was the kind of thing you said to a poodle who'd fetched you the newspaper. Except that she didn't get the pat on the head.

Twenty minutes later, however, she was at Bretannia's getting a proper reception from a beaming Alex. He wore a khaki shirt that needed pressing and an unseasonably hot tweed jacket. A medal rather like the dog tags soldiers wore peeked out now and then at his open collar.

He'd already ordered "American" for them both, he announced—hamburgers with everything. He ate with great appetite, laughing readily and making her feel as if she'd known him forever. He'd lived in the States much of his life, as he'd told her before, mostly in St. Louis, and to their delight, they discovered that they'd attended the same high school.

Penny, feeling comfortable with him, told him about her parents' divorce, about her mother's upcoming marriage, about her father's dangerous life-style and about the loss of the childhood home she loved.

"'When sorrows come, they come not single spies,'" he quoted, "'but in battalions.'"

"You had Mrs. Goff for English, too," she said, remembering how the teacher had always recited that line from *Hamlet*.

"As a matter of fact, I didn't. A great many people find that particular thought fitting and commit it to memory, I'd guess."

"I suppose you're right."

"If you leave Athens, it won't be for good," he predicted, suddenly serious. "You'll be back. You can't spade out Greek roots so easily and throw them away. There's always a piece you've missed and it shoots up again. Like ivy."

"Maybe." Her eyes burned with unshed tears.

If Alex noticed, he didn't mention it. "When you come back, promise to look me up. We might still be able to arrange something."

"I promise. That reminds me. I brought a few sketches I thought might interest you. Ideas I had this morning that I thought might work for your new line."

He stuck out his lower lip and nodded. "I saw that about you right away. The brain never stops clicking." He undid the clasp on the manila envelope she'd handed him, drew the papers out and studied them. His eyes twinkled as he looked at her, then back at the papers. "Not much visual appeal here, Penny. And the copy is much too wordy."

"Wordy?" She scooted her chair close to his and read:

SUBJECT: Environmental impact
PROJECT: Proposed Zone Amendment

"Oh, no!" She threw a hand over her mouth in horror.

"You picked up the wrong papers, I presume."

"You don't know *how* wrong. This is... Oh, Alex, I have to run. I don't have time to explain." She started to get up, saw Steffan heading across the room toward her, and sank into her chair again.

He looked more tired than angry, and he carried the briefcase she'd given him. How far had he gone into his meeting before he noticed her mistake? Had her swimsuit drawings been passed around the conference table?

"These are yours, I imagine." He held out the sketches. "And those are mine."

Penny's cheeks burned as he took the report from her. Mental pictures of her actions, from the moment she picked up the briefcase until she handed it to Steffan at the hotel, ran through her mind. "I can't imagine how this happened. I remember distinctly—"

"It doesn't matter how it happened." Steffan scanned the papers hurriedly, before sliding them into his case.

"How did you find me?"

"Fortunately Wanda remembered what you told her."

"Steffan, there's no way I could possibly have made such a mistake."

"Obviously you did." She heard no bitterness in his voice, only resignation, as if such mistakes were all he could expect from her.

"What about your conference?"

"It's been rescheduled."

"Would you care to join us?" Alex asked, somewhat puzzled by the exchange.

"No, thank you." Steffan didn't look at him.

"I'm sorry," Penny said, almost wishing he would lose his temper. His patience was harder to bear. "Is there anything I can do?"

"Finish your meal. We'll thrash this out later."

"Everyone makes mistakes," Alex told her after Steffan had gone and Penny explained the situation briefly. "He seemed like a reasonable guy. He understands."

"What he understands is that he's stuck with a bubblehead. And I'd planned to be the indispensable Girl Friday he'd bemoan losing. Now he'll probably break out a bottle of champagne when I turn in my notice. This is the second meeting he's had to cancel because of me."

"'When sorrows come,'" Alex said, "'they come not single spies...'"

"'...but in battalions,'" she finished for him. "What next?"

Lon was home in time for dinner as Penny had requested, and they would eat together—but not in the privacy of their own quarters and not alone. The Korda cook was preparing *pastitsio*, a macaroni in bechamel sauce that was among her father's favorite dishes, and not to be missed come forest fire or hurricane.

It was pleasant in the green-and-white dining room, with its polished cherrywood, its hanging planters and the floor-to-ceiling windows looking onto the garden. The food was as delicious as Lon had promised, and he delighted the woman who served them by raving over each mouthful and pressing his fingers to his lips in ecstasy.

Steffan hadn't returned from the city yet, so there were only the three of them at dinner—Penny, her father and Wanda, who looked especially nice, with her hair drawn back and a small curl fixed over each ear. She'd caught too much sun that day, though, and her skin was painfully red in contrast to the stark white of her sleeveless dress.

She was especially talkative, too, just as she'd been especially friendly at work that day. Perhaps she was nervous about the angry words they had exchanged in the garden the night before, Penny thought. She knew she'd said too much and was hoping Penny wouldn't tell her father.

She chattered on about the driving habits of Athenians and how the accident rate in Greece was the highest in the world. She talked about *okhi*, the Greek word for "no" and how it still confused her after all the time she'd been here. "I keep thinking they're saying 'okay.'"

Then she talked about Omaha, Nebraska, where she'd lived as a child, and about coming to Greece with a tour group. She had loved it so much she'd vowed to return when she could afford it.

She'd managed to get a job some years later as secretary to a government official and all had been well until her employer decided to retire several months before, because of poor health. She hadn't wanted to go back to Nebraska, but hadn't found any suitable employment, and her funds were shrinking rapidly. Luckily she'd met Lon and through him, got the job with Steffan.

"I must say, I wasn't looking too hard for work," she admitted. "There must be something in the air or the water here that turns industrious little ants into butterflies."

If her nonstop patter annoyed Lon, he didn't let on. He smiled in the right places, nodded, and even added a tale or two of his own about how he and Wanda had met. He'd come to her rescue when the boat she and a party of her friends had chartered sprung a leak. She glowed with the telling, hanging on to each of his words, and Penny wondered how Lon could not be aware of how much the woman cared for him.

Or maybe he was.

As to his feelings for Wanda, Penny couldn't hazard a guess. It was becoming more and more apparent that he enjoyed her company. And she suspected he'd grown dependent on Wanda for moral support. But watching the two of them together didn't tell her much. Her father had never been demonstrative. Open displays of affection embarrassed him. And hinting for an answer wouldn't have worked. He was an expert dodger.

If Penny wanted to know about the relationship, she'd have to come right out and ask him, and she couldn't see herself doing that. Not when he already thought she was meddling in his life.

When there was finally a lull in the conversation, she leapt into it, talking enthusiastically about Constance and the shop and reminding her father of people and places he hadn't seen for a very long time.

"I imagine it would be fun for you to visit some of your old haunts and look up some of the boys you went to school with."

"It would at that," he admitted, "if I ever found the time."

"There's always time if you look for it."

"I suppose so."

"They say some of the gold shipments Jesse James and his brother buried were never found," Penny teased. "Maybe we can do some research on it and come up lucky."

"Maybe we could." He chuckled. "My daughter, the prospector. Wouldn't that be a picture?"

Wanda laughed, too, but it was a hollow laugh, without mirth.

Penny wasn't entirely comfortable, either, but for an entirely different reason. Steffan could put in an appearance at any time, and after today's mix-up, she wasn't eager to face him.

It put a damper on the good news she'd been hoping to share with her father at dinner. Alex had liked her work. He was looking for a softer approach for that particular line, but thought her idea could be adapted to Sun Dial's new swimsuits for the younger crowd, and told her to get at it. He'd readily accepted her offer to take now-and-then assignments and had sent her home loaded down with catalogs.

Such news wasn't to be tossed casually around the table before moving on to something else. She'd wait until morning and tell her father about it over coffee, when she had his full attention.

After the dishes were cleared away and they'd had dessert, Wanda challenged Lon to a game of backgammon that went on and on. Penny decided to go for a swim.

With a striped towel over one shoulder, and decked out in a new white one-piece swimsuit, she found her way to the pool. Few things could calm her nerves and bring her back to herself the way swimming did—knifing through the cool water, taking laps, one after the other, without counting them, then turning onto her back with her eyes closed and only the barest flutter of her feet to keep her afloat.

Swimming had been her passion since she'd discovered it at the age of two, and the closest she'd ever come to a serious romantic entanglement had been with her partner in a water ballet in college. There was something undeniably sensual about the perfectly matched fluid movements of their bodies through the jade-green water, and she'd fancied herself in love. He'd been blond and bronzed, with a small gap in the front of his otherwise perfect teeth. All their friends raved about how wonderful they looked together. Then the semester ended. The water ballet was no more. With their feet on dry land, they found they had nothing to talk about.

Still caught up in the memory, Penny stepped out of her thongs onto the smooth paving stones and discovered too late that Steffan had not only returned, but had opted for a dip in the pool instead of a dish of *pastitsio*.

If she could have retreated, she would have. But he'd seen her. If she could have pretended she was there searching for a missing lipstick, she would have. But the swimsuit and towel gave away her intentions.

Pasting on a smile she hoped would pass for pleasant surprise, she walked casually to the edge of the pool and looked down at him. He reached for the tile edging and gave his head a shake to clear his vision.

"Come in. The water couldn't be better."

"I can tell by looking."

"No, you can't. And you were never content to sit on the sidelines, I remember."

"What do you remember?" she asked, stalling.

"Oh." He shook his head again to throw a lock of hair into place, but it flopped back over his forehead. "I remember you were a serious swimmer. A little girl who always seemed to be trying to win a race. Even when she was alone."

Because of Lon's friendship, Basil had given Penny blanket permission to use the pool; but for a long time, Constance wouldn't allow it, wanting nothing from the Kordas. During her twelfth and thirteenth years however, Penny, whose infatuation with Steffan was in full bloom, had begged and finally won.

Often she'd see Steffan on the terrace with his books or sitting at his upstairs bedroom window. In her efforts to impress him with her skill, she'd probably seemed driven.

"I remember a red polka-dot swimsuit you always wore," he went on. "It was all ruffles—here." He grinned and made elaborate gestures across his chest. "I used to wonder how you moved so well with all that fancy trimming. I would have thought it would get in your way."

Penny sank to her knees, then shifted to a sitting position and allowed her fingers to play in the water. She'd had a straight, immature figure until she was almost sixteen. She'd specifically bought the suit Steffan described because she thought the ruffles might help camouflage her embarrassing lack of feminine curves.

Soaking wet, with his hair dripping in his face, his chest and shoulders glistening, minus the trappings of wealth and success, he seemed to be a man like any other. He didn't look authoritative. He only looked appealing.

"How about a race right now?" she blurted, wanting to drive the past back into the shadowy corners of her memory where it belonged.

He groaned and held up his hands. "You have me at a disadvantage. I've already been at it for fifteen minutes. I was about to get out."

"We'll call that a handicap."

"From what I remember of the little girl in the ruffled suit, the handicap would be on the wrong side."

"Excuses, excuses."

He shrugged. "Very well. You're on."

Pushing off, they collided forcefully now and then. They swam, sometimes shoulder to shoulder, sometimes with Penny in the lead, sometimes with Steffan well ahead. He was a strong swimmer, she knew. But she was better. She fully expected to win. It was a victory she wanted badly. But it wasn't hers. Steffan's strokes were relaxed and sure. She had tried too hard.

With easy grace he pushed up and out of the pool and stood looking down at her. The brevity of his plain black swimming shorts allowed her a striking view of his superb physique. His shoulders and arms were thicker and more powerful looking than they'd been in his youth. The muscles of his calves and thighs more strongly developed.

Laughing, he thrust a hand at her and she caught it, allowing herself to be hoisted out of the water and into his arms. His eyes looked steadily into hers and she didn't flinch. Seconds ticked by inside her brain, and it seemed as if both of them were waiting for some signal from the other.

"With your hair wet like this and without your lipstick, you still look like that little girl." His hands smoothed her arms down to the elbows, leaving chill bumps in their wake, and his eyes took the same path, missing nothing along the way. "Well, not so little." His mouth pulled down at one corner with his teasing. "No need for ruffles these days."

The ruffles. He'd known the reason for them all along. Feeling her face flush, she stepped away and reached for her towel. He took it from her and began to rub her shoulders briskly.

"You look cold. I'm having something to eat. Would you care to join me?"

"I've already eaten."

"Melon, berries, sweet cakes," he coaxed.

"Nothing, thank you."

He pressed her into a chair, signaled to one of the servants hovering in the doorway, then caught up his own towel and wrapped it around his shoulders. "Keep me company anyway. If you want to try racing another day, I usually swim every evening. It helps clear my head."

"Surprise. We have something in common." She made a small circling motion with one index finger.

He didn't smile. "Maybe not such a surprise. Do you like to walk? I don't mean once or twice around the grounds, I mean *walk*. Of course, you do," he said, before she could answer. "You got yourself lost on Skopelos that day in your enthusiasm for it. We'll take a walk, you and I. Soon. Up Parnassus, maybe. It's a good climb, without being too demanding, and there's Delphi to see. Do you know it?"

She felt giddy with all the attention he was giving her. He was just being friendly, she reminded herself. He was helping to entertain the daughter of a dear friend. He believed it was safe to spend time with her now that he'd had his say and warned her not to expect anything from their relationship.

Still, the ache of denying what she felt between them spread through her quickly and settled around her heart. "The place of the oracle," she said too brightly. "The center of the earth."

"Yes. It's picturesque and lovely. We'll go there one day. Right now, the business is stirring. We're experiencing upheaval, with property changing hands and all of us working twenty-four-hour days. But we'll plan our trip soon. When everything's settled."

She nodded, knowing it wouldn't happen. She couldn't let it happen. "I'd better go in now."

"Tomorrow will be better," he promised solemnly. "Your job, I mean."

"Better?"

"As you learn the routine. Typing correspondence will make up much of your work. So it might be a good idea if you allow Wanda to show you how to run the dictaphone machine."

"I know how to run it already."

"Oh?" He frowned slightly. "Then you didn't have time to finish the letters I dictated today."

She adjusted her towel where the stretchy terry of her swimsuit had slipped below the line of her tan. "I finished them and put them in the basket for your signature."

"Two of them were in the basket. Two—the most important two—were not. No matter. You likely took my hesitation for the end of the tape."

"No," she shot back. "I distinctly remember four letters. They—"

"Don't fret about it." He concentrated on his chair arms, not looking at her. "It was partly my fault. A new job. My pressing you into action so quickly. Then, last night—"

She'd expected the comment and pounced on it. "Last night had nothing to do with this."

"Making a mistake on your first day is perfectly understandable."

"Why? Beause I'm an overemotional female who gets so flustered by a bit of masculine attention that I completely lose my head?"

"I'm trying to be nice, Penelope."

"Don't be nice. Be yourself."

"All right, then." His head snapped up. "Dammit. The first step toward getting into the scheme of things is to take responsibility for your own actions. We're friends here."

"I don't mind taking responsibility when . . ." Her voice trailed off as she realized how she must have sounded.

Wanda could have swept up the letters accidently and mixed them with the great flood of papers she'd been searching through. It was also possible, she thought bleakly, that Steffan had whisked them away to make her feel inadequate. In any case, they were gone.

"I'm sorry," she managed. "I can go in and type those letters now. It won't take long."

"The mail's already gone. I took care of it by telephone." He pressed back in his chair and the hardness faded from his expression. "No harm done. Just be more careful from now on."

Oh, I will, she said silently as she retreated. Her suit had ridden up at the bottom, uncovering a bit more skin than she would have liked. She could imagine where Steffan's gaze had fallen, but she wouldn't give him the satisfaction of any self-conscious adjustment.

From now on, she promised, *I check and double-check. Nothing gets by me. Absolutely nothing.*

CHAPTER NINE

WANDA, WHO WORE an eye-popping mustard-yellow tunic over white pants, greeted Penny with enthusiasm. It would be a nonstop day, she promised, and started right in.

"You'll find that Steffan hasn't actually composed today's letters. He's given you the gist of what he wants said, and expects you to supply the wording. Here's a folder of examples, in case you think it might help."

"I see." Penny nodded and flipped through the letters.

"When you're finished, put them in the upper basket on the right-hand side of his desk. If he approves them, they'll be in the upper basket on the left-hand side. If he doesn't, you'll find them on your desk with notations in red, telling you what has to be changed."

Penny blew out her cheeks. Left-hand basket. Right-hand basket. "The red is blood, I take it?"

"I wouldn't be surprised."

"Where is he now?" Penny stressed "he," as if it referred to a sleeping giant.

Wanda pointed a finger at the closed door. "In there. And speaking of blood, let me warn you. When the door is shut, don't enter. Don't even knock, unless the house is on fire."

"And not then," Penny added, "if I can manage to smother the flames with my body."

Wanda made a circle of thumb and forefinger and they laughed together.

They sobered quickly however, when the door opened and Steffan looked out. "Wanda, has Garrett Wheeler called?"

"No."

"Dammit. Have you tried to locate him?"

"In all the probable places."

"Try the improbable ones. It's imperative that I talk to him now."

"Yes, sir."

"And hold my other calls."

"Is this Garrett Wheeler another important out-of-towner?" Penny asked, when Steffan had disappeared.

"Out-of-towner, no. Important? Yes, yes, yes. He's one of the Big Three."

"That certainly sounds important, but what does it mean?"

Wanda took a deep breath and glanced toward the door as if she were about to divulge a state secret. "The Big Three. Basil Korda, Garrett Wheeler, and Yuri Stravos. You'll meet Yuri. He's a lovely sweet man. Anyway, the three of them were partners many, many years ago. They bought their first hotel, the Wayfarer, together, because none of them was rich enough to manage it alone."

"Later when all three had made their fortunes, each of them tried to buy the other two out, as a symbol of success, I suppose. The problem was that none of them would give in. So the Wayfarer stayed divided among the three. It really infuriated Basil Korda. He never gave up trying. Not even at the end."

"And now?"

"Yuri is willing to sell his third. He has a sick wife and wants to retire to spend more time with her."

"And Garrett Wheeler?"

"The present Mr. Wheeler is the son and heir. He and Steffan despise each other with a passion. He isn't really a hotel man. I think he held on to his part of the hotel just out of spite."

"But Steffan thinks he's ready to give in?"

Wanda nodded. "The word is that Garrett Wheeler is in dire need of cash. All his funds are tied up, so he's ready to make a deal. That could change at any time and Steffan is terrified that he'll get his hands on the money he needs elsewhere and the sale will be off.''

So Steffan was still trying to prove himself to his father, even though the old man was gone, Penny mused. "Garrett Wheeler," she repeated to reinforce it in her memory. Just as long as getting in touch with him didn't mean another gala evening of nightclubbing. She couldn't survive it.

Steffan's promise that she'd earn every penny of her salary hadn't been exaggerated. Things were so hectic, there was no time for lunch. She barely noticed. Mostly she was grateful she had no direct dealings with the Big Boss. Every so often he came out to ask about Wheeler, but that was all. Miraculously her letters were all approved. They'd been left in the out-basket for mailing without a single correction. It gave her the same kind of feeling she'd had in the second grade when she received an A in a spelling test.

Her most difficult hours were spent when Wanda left to do some errands. Steffan was having coffee on the terrace with some hotel staff members and she had to take over the phones. Orders were that nobody was to get through except the elusive Mr. Wheeler.

Most people were understanding about being put off. Others were more insistent. A woman with a throaty, movie-actress sort of voice called every half hour and wanted to wait on the line each time. She wouldn't say why her call was so urgent, and she wouldn't leave a number. Another woman took it as a personal affront that Mr. Korda didn't make himself available to her. "I'll have your name, my girl," she sniffed. "Then I can tell Mr. Korda who refused to put my call through."

A man who introduced himself as Yuri Stravos called to confirm an appointment he had with Steffan on the twenty-third and Penny recognized his name as being one of the Big Three.

"He's to come for a meal," the man said in a voice that might have belonged to "the Godfather." He added, "My wife says to remind him to bring his appetite."

Though from what Penny knew of Steffan's appetite, he never went anywhere without it, she made careful note on a memo slip and promised to relay the message.

Her next caller introduced himself as Sonny. He was pleasant, but hardest of all to discourage. "So you're the new little lady he has runing interference for him. Are you as much of a cutie as you sound?"

Penny cringed. "I don't know how to answer that, sir."

"None of that 'sir' business. Call me Sonny. Now that we're friends, admit it. The guy's sitting there tossing playing cards into a trash can, isn't he?"

"No, he isn't."

"Maybe you're even sitting on his lap. I really need a quick word with him. How about it?"

"I'm sorry. Will you leave a message?"

"Sure you can't put me through?"

"He isn't here."

"Well, I'll be at Le Foyer another, oh, fifteen minutes. If I don't hear from him by then, I'll split. What are you doing tonight, by the way?"

Penny scribbled "Sonny" and "Le Foyer" on the message pad. "I have plans," she said.

"Sure you wouldn't consider changing those plans for a fun-filled evening with a charming, handsome, athletic type who's already hooked by your voice?"

"I'm sorry, Mr. er, Mr...."

"Sonny."

"Sonny," she repeated, humoring him.

No sooner had she hung up than Wanda popped in, out of breath, with the welcome news that Penny could close up shop and go home. "I have a few odds and ends to take care of here after Steffan comes back, but then I'm going to take a break, too."

"What about the phones?"

"I'll turn on the answering machine."

"Mr. Wheeler might call."

Wanda shook her head. "It's almost four. Garrett Wheeler wouldn't lift a pen after four if it meant losing a ten-million-dollar deal. It's hard policy with him. Get a good rest now. You'll need your strength tomorrow."

The sky was cloudless and a vivid blue. Chittering sparrows were joyfully taking advantage of the birdbath in the garden.

"Lucky for you little guys," Penny told them as she paused to watch, "that Steffan's mother wasn't a bird fancier. You'd have been evicted, too, like the goldfish."

Her father was out, but he'd left her a message that Constance had called. "She's fine," he'd scribbled. "Just wanted to know how you're doing."

Penny had already tried several times to get a call through to St. Louis. But except for the one she'd made the first day, to let Constance know she'd arrived safely, she'd been unsuccessful. Now that her mother wasn't at the shop during the day and Kenneth was taking her out to dinner and to unlikely places like bingo games and stock-car races at night, it was hard to guess when she'd be home.

So her father and mother had spoken, Penny mused, as she tried a call of her own. For the first time in more than a year. She couldn't help but wonder about the tone of the conversation. The last one, as she recalled from months ago, had gone from start to finish without bitterness or sarcasm, at least on her mother's part.

"Your father!" Constance had said, laughing, as she'd hung up. "They say everybody has a twin somewhere, but I'll never believe that's true where he's concerned." There'd been warmth in her voice. Her face had been flushed and her eyes bright as those of a schoolgirl.

When there was no answer now after the tenth ring, Penny hung up. She'd try again later.

After the air-conditioning in the main house, she felt especially warm in the guest house and decided to change into a pair of shorts and a halter top. She'd lie on the chaise longue in the secluded grassy area next to the bedroom, catch what remained of the afternoon sun and look over the catalogs Alex had given her.

Where were they? Oh, yes. She'd put them in the drawer of the telephone stand.

She sat cross-legged on the floor, humming to herself. At first she couldn't find what she was looking for. Her father had put some papers on top of them. Letters. Charts. Maps. She sorted through them hurriedly, praying they were old ones. They weren't. The manila envelope was marked with yesterday's date. The map showed an area between Naxos and Amorgos in the Cyclades island group. It was marked with squiggly lines and symbols, making it all but unintelligible to the average person. But Penny wasn't the average person. She'd learned to decipher such maps before she'd learned to follow the adventures of Dick, Jane and Baby Sally. She spread it on the floor and studied it with growing agitation.

"Got a search warrant, copper?" her father asked in a pretty good imitation of James Cagney.

"Oh, Daddy," was the only thing she could say. "What is all this?"

"What does it look like?" He skittered past her to the kitchen.

Wanda trailed after him, carrying a bulging bag of groceries. She formed a silent hello with her lips and made a swipe across her forehead with the back of her hand. "It's even hotter in here than it is outside, if that's possible."

"The heat is good for whatever ails you." Lon looked stronger today. Or perhaps he'd readied himself to do battle. "I could never figure out why people pay good money to toast themselves in a sauna bath. Then they rush home to turn on the refrigeration."

"Is that what you're trying to do?" Wanda asked. "Turn this place into a sauna bath?"

Penny thumped her knuckles against the map. "What's supposed to be here? King Solomon's Mines?"

"Better than that, baby." Lon winked. "Because it's accessible. Let's put these things away and I'll tell you about it. I didn't before, because you always get so wrought-up like your ma. But you gotta keep it under your wig."

"Who would I tell? Who would be remotely interested?"

"A hell of a lot of people, that's who. A hell of a lot of people."

According to his theory, no one was immune to the lure of treasure. Not tax collectors, librarians or insurance salesmen. Penny waited, but it wasn't easy. She even listened without interrupting, as he related a story about a man who'd made a fortune smuggling jewelry and art objects out of France and England in the twenties and thirties. Then he'd gone to one of the Greek islands to wait out the war and to enjoy the fruits of his thievery.

In 1943 he got nervous about the encroaching German occupation, and about guerilla action. He and some trusted servants crated up the most valuable of his possessions and took them out in a boat, figuring to move them to a cave he knew about on one of the more remote islands. But a boat had appeared from nowhere, and the crates were slid over the side. He marked the area and planned to come back when it was safe, but he died before he could manage it. One of the servants was the grandfather of Eugenie Minotis, Nikko's wife. The old man had kept the map, but was too superstitious and fearful to do anything about it, and he'd eventually passed it on to Nikko.

"Exciting, isn't it?" Wanda said with a sigh. "Imagine not only finding something of value, but something with a history of smuggling, intrigue and war."

"Nikko wants a thousand dollars," Lon went on. "If I can come up with it, I'm a full partner."

Nikko, the bear-man. She might have known she hadn't heard the last of him. "Why should Nikko have approached you with this story?" Penny asked.

Lon rolled his eyes at Wanda and snorted. "Will you listen to my daughter? She doesn't realize how well-known I am in the world of treasure hunters."

"I'm prepared to believe you're extremely well-known." Penny cast a look at Wanda for support, but the woman was staring at Lon as if he'd just discovered a cure for the heretofore uncurable. "You're well-known as a good listener to unlikely tales."

"Nikko has been approached by a string of others who are dying for a peek at this map." His voice was building in intensity. "He wanted to give me first crack."

"If the existence of this treasure is such a dark secret, why do so many people know about it?"

"Rumors, little girl, rumors. Only hard facts count."

"Hard facts. So you hand Nikko your thousand dollars and he sells you some swampland in Florida—or excuse me, a treasure that *might* be there."

"Poke fun at your old man if you want. You won't be the first." He walked over to switch on the television, letting her know the discussion was over.

"And the other money you'll need?" Penny persisted. "The money for the boat and diving equipment? Where will you get it?"

"I'll get it."

From Steffan. Penny stared at the flickering screen. A giant reptile was devouring a city. She didn't say any more.

CHAPTER TEN

STEFFAN WASN'T IN HIS OFFICE or on the terrace. He wasn't in the library, either, though the maid had told her he might be. At least, Penny didn't see him at first. The door was ajar and the room had an empty feel to it. But as she started away in exasperation, something made her take another look. He was at the window, lost in thought.

From somewhere far off a dog barked, and he stirred, conscious of her for the first time. His lips parted in surprise.

"How did your day go?" he asked, his sweeping glance making her conscious of the scanty sunbathing costume she wore.

"Busy," she said. "But I like to keep busy."

"Good. Then you'll like your job." As he came closer, her blood began to simmer. There was shared hunger in the silence that fell between them. "You haven't been here very long. Who was the man you were with at Bretannia's?" His question was hesitant, as though he knew his right to ask it might be challenged.

"He represents a company I'd expected to work for here."

He scowled. "I wouldn't have guessed he was a business acquaintance. You appeared to be more like old friends."

"Alex is one of those people who are easy to know."

"Alex," he repeated. "Mmm." He reached out to pluck something from her hair. It was a leaf.

Instinctively she flinched. His hand brushed her cheek and the touch of it was like a brand. Intense heat spread over the side of her face and down her neck. "I took a shortcut through the garden," she explained.

The dog barked again and he looked toward the sound. "I never hear a dog bark without thinking of Gus."

"My Gus?"

"In some ways he was my Gus, too. You had a funeral for him in your backyard when he died. Flowers, prayers. You even sang."

"You saw?"

He nodded. "I wept for him myself. In private. He used to come along with us on the boat sometimes. I taught him to roll over and walk on his hind legs."

"You taught him those things? I thought he had a high I.Q. and picked them up by himself." Her fingers curled more tightly around the rolled up map as she was seized with a wild longing to touch him. A phantom Penny stepped invisibly forward on tiptoe to press bold lips against his.

No. She didn't want to shape any more dreams around him. She didn't want to talk about Gus. With her sense of purpose reinforced, she walked past him and spread the map on his desk, accidently knocking a paper knife to the floor.

"This is an area in the Cyclades..." she said, stooping to retrieve the knife.

Her voice faltered as Steffan reached for it at the same time and they very nearly collided. She set it down hurriedly, too close to the edge. It fell again. This time she allowed him to put it right.

"This is an area in the Cyclades," she repeated.

"So it is." A smile played on his lips.

She stepped back to put room between them, smoothed the map again and used her finger to trace the line someone had drawn with a red marker. "You already know that my father is prepared to spend money he doesn't have trying to bring up treasure."

"Yes, I know."

"I came here to ask you not to encourage him in this. He won't be able to see it through if you don't lend him the money."

"He's already asked me and I've already agreed."

"Tell him you've changed your mind."

"Isn't this the same conversation we had the day you arrived?"

"Practically."

"Then you know how I feel." His voice was low, but braced with iron. "Penny, your father won't be crushed if he fails, because he isn't alone. He has us. And he has Wanda now, too."

"Wanda." She rolled her eyes ceilingward.

"You don't like her?" His look was quizzical.

Had he asked her that question two days ago, she would have answered a resounding no. Now she couldn't. The woman was likable. They might even have been friends under less trying circumstances. Wanda was intelligent, she had a good sense of humor and she didn't put on airs though Penny thought the woman's feelings for Lon had clouded her judgment.

"I don't know what to think about her," Penny answered honestly. "If my father took up race-car driving or skydiving she'd applaud. She doesn't want to risk his disapproval by crossing him, even if it means his life."

"She might behave differently if she thought she could stop him."

"I doubt it. If she truly had his best interests at heart, she'd—"

"Walk out on him?" Steffan shot back.

Penny waited the traditional count to ten before saying anything. She knew the reasons behind Steffan's bitterness and how he'd come to believe that women simply walked out when everything wasn't rosy. She shouldn't take it personally.

"What about me and my peace of mind?" she asked softly. "Do you—all of you—expect me to sit back and smile while my father moves from one life-risking adventure to another? Am I supposed to clink glasses with you and say, 'Here's hoping he makes it out alive this time?' Steffan, don't I count?"

"You count very much." He lifted one hand to stroke her hair—slowly, as if he feared she might object—and she sensed an overpowering tenderness in his touch. She almost believed him.

"Then tell him you've changed your mind about the financing."

"No. I can't allow my feelings for you to pressure me into making what I consider an unfair decision."

My feelings for you. His words swirled around inside her head, taking on more and more meaning. *My feelings for you.*

She didn't want to quarrel with him. She wanted to glide into the circle of his arms and stay there. She wanted to touch her lips to the familiar roughness of his tanned cheek and feel his breath on her ear as he whispered reassurances. But he was wrong. So wrong. "Please," she said.

"I can't."

His refusal to be reasonable gave her the jolt of strength she needed. She raised her head to look at him with new-found determination. "You pretend to care for him, yet you allow him to build up hopes, when you know perfectly well they'll be crushed and he'll be worse off than ever. He'll be deeper and deeper in debt to you and he'll have to continue trying to pay you off. He'll end up throwing his life away—if he survives—just to satisfy some need you have for vicarious excitement."

"Stop it." He caught her shoulders gently. "You're upsetting yourself. I'm no adventurer—"

"You're an armchair adventurer," she insisted, wanting to make him angry. At least anger was honest, and she could deal with it more easily.

But he wasn't angry. It was as though he'd come to a decision not to blow up at her, no matter what she said. Her provocations, her entreaties, were useless. When she began to weep softly, he sighed and cradled her against him, swaying slightly.

She didn't protest his holding her. She couldn't.

"The last thing I want is to see you hurt," he said, then pulled away slightly to look fully into her face, his dark eyes probing hers, as though he hoped to transfer his thoughts to her mind. "Nothing's worth that." With hesitant fingers, he brushed at her tears. Trailing down her jaw, his hand came to rest under her chin. "Nothing."

As his thumb continued its quest and found her lower lip, she wondered if he could feel the throbbing fever there. He traced its velvety contour, then drew his thumb down to edge her teeth and slip between them to reach her tongue. He tensed at the contact, and suddenly his lips swooped down in its stead. One hand applied growing pressure to her back to bring her close. The other, still at her chin, held her steady.

"Help me," she cried breathlessly, as his lips scorched hers.

"You know I will," he said. "I promise your father won't be hurt."

"Oh! Excuse me." Wanda stood in the doorway, her face scarlet to the roots of her hair. She stared intently at her notepad she was carrying.

"What is it?" Steffan asked tersely, after taking a moment to find his voice.

"I have a question. Penelope," she said, her eyes still averted. "This message you took. It says 'Sonny called.'"

"He did."

"Good lord." Steffan moved quickly toward Wanda. He snatched the notepad away and read it. "Are you telling me that Garrett Wheeler actually telephoned and you didn't put him through?"

"Garrett Wheeler? No." Penny looked from Steffan to Wanda and back to Steffan again. "That is ... you mean ... Sonny is—"

"Where is he now?" Steffan interrupted, as if it took great effort on his part to keep from strangling her.

"The note mentions Le Foyer," Wanda suggested. "Was he phoning from there?"

"Yes."

"Le Foyer." Steffan slapped a hand to the back of his neck. "Have him called to the phone."

"He said he'd be there only fifteen minutes."

Wanda, who'd started toward the outer office, froze almost comically. "And when was that?"

"Hours ago," Penny said hesitantly.

Steffan threw up his hands. "Didn't you ever take messages at this company you worked for in St. Louis?"

"Yes, but—"

"Did he say anything else?" Wanda broke in.

"He asked me to go out with him tonight."

"That figures," Steffan growled. "And?"

"I told him I had other plans."

He muttered something under his breath and turned away.

"I'll call Le Foyer anyway," Wanda offered. "He might have left a clue as to where he was going next."

"No one told me he might use a nickname."

"And no one told you that he likes his steaks rare, or that he was born in Fresno, California." Steffan shook his head. "Didn't you think to ask for his full name?"

"Yes, but he insisted I call him Sonny."

"He insisted," Steffan mocked with ill-concealed fury.

Wanda crooked her little finger and beckoned for Penny to follow her out of the room. Obviously she thought it best to leave him alone until he simmered down.

"I should have known better," Penny wailed. Angry as she was at Steffan's unfairness, she was angrier still at herself. She'd sworn that nothing would get by her. And now she'd unwittingly made a third mistake—the most serious yet.

"Well, I wish I'd thought to clue you in on this 'Sonny' thing," Wanda said. "But he doesn't use it often anymore.

Only when he's in a playful mood, as he must be today, hearing a new voice on the phone, seeing a chance to make a conquest. Cheer up. It's your first week.''

"And probably my last."

"You're Lon's daughter. Steffan wouldn't fire you if you tore the building down around our ears."

"I don't want to hold a job that way."

"Forget it. Steffan will."

"Fat chance."

Not a leaf rustled in the canopy of branches overhead as Penny stepped from one whitewashed stone to the other on her way to the guest cottage. A gray squirrel made a chattering sound as if it were scolding her, too, and streaked for cover into the azalea bushes ahead.

Sonny, alias Garrett Wheeler, was somewhere in the city. Should she take the car and try to ferret him out on her own? If she could convince him to set aside his rule against business "after hours" and call Steffan tonight, it might not keep her from looking inefficient, but it would undo the damage she'd unintentionally done.

If he was a regular patron at Le Foyer—wherever that was—maybe Penny could begin there. He didn't sound like the kind of man who went unnoticed, keeping his comings and goings secret.

She stopped walking. The Saab was in the garage. Should she . . . ? No, she'd better not, she decided. Considering the direction her judgment had taken of late, she'd probably end up in even deeper trouble than she was already.

Better to sit back and try to forget the whole day by concentrating on another idea for her Sun Dial presentation. She wanted to have it ready for her next meeting with Alex. Despite the turmoil of the day, a few possibilities were buzzing around inside her head and she wanted to get them on paper.

"So you're not a fashion model," she murmured to herself, imagining the ad. "You're not a movie star. You're better. You're *you*, in a Sun Dial swimsuit."

She began to walk again.

The next morning's mail brought the first letter from Constance Haywood since Penny's arrival in Glyfada. Except for missing her "darling" daughter, she was having a glorious time as a lady of leisure. She didn't miss going to the shop at all. Sleeping late was a luxury she could get used to. She'd bought herself a beautiful new wardrobe just for her trip and had decided against going to Hawaii.

"Don't be disappointed," she wrote. "I know you wanted me to go. But I've never been a good traveler and there's so much to do right here. Kenneth is so cute, and so much fun. We have a good time wherever we are."

Penny reread the letter over her breakfast of orange juice and toast, remembering the boisterous laugh that caused heads to turn. The close-set hazel eyes. The stale jokes with the forgotten punch lines. The atrocious crocheted ties. These things were Kenneth Glass, her mother's beau. He was kind, yes. He was sweet, maybe. But cute? Fun? Penny grimaced and shook her head. After all these years of being alone, Constance had hypnotized herself into seeing him as the little man on the wedding cake. It was sad.

Her father, sitting opposite her and working on the newspaper crossword puzzle as he did every morning, pushed the paper aside and heaved a deep sigh of defeat. "Damn. I've yet to finish one of these blasted things. Somebody must, or they wouldn't keep printing 'em. Makes me feel like a pea brain."

"Some were born to build bridges," Penny sang out, still contemplating her letter, "others to invent new kinds of computer games. And some were born to finish crossword puzzles."

"And me?" Lon tapped his pencil on the table. "What was I born to do?"

"Anything you put your mind to," she said, suddenly earnest. "You could—"

"Try the strawberry jam," Lon interrupted, side-stepping the coming lecture. He pushed the jar toward her.

"Wanda gets it from a woman on the north side who puts up her own."

Wanda! Penny thought with a sigh. Was there anything he hadn't grown to depend on her for? "What are you planning to do today?" she asked quickly, disturbed at her feelings of resentment toward the woman. After all, Wanda had been trying so hard lately to be helpful.

"Oh, a thing or two."

His evasion had already given her an answer. "Name one."

"Now, baby," he drawled. "We're getting along too good to get into a row about you-know-what. Let's just say I'll be busy and leave it at that. I guess you'll be busy, too. Working today, are you?"

"Yes, and I'd better go." She drank the last of her orange juice and carried the breakfast things to the sink. She'd wash them later. There was no point in adding tardiness to her growing list of shortcomings.

A hollow stillness greeted her at the office, and before she even opened the door, she guessed correctly that no one was there. A propped-up note told her that Steffan was gone for the day and Wanda would be tied up at the Korda Inn. The duties Penny had been asked to perform in their absence were ones that didn't require much judgment or know-how—straightening the file cabinets, watering plants, photocopying, stapling, and sending out form letters. She could leave, she was informed, when all were checked off. The answering machine had been left on, so she wouldn't even have to bother with the phone.

Mindless as the jobs were, they were time-consuming and it was nearly three o'clock before she came to the last of them. She heard the single ring, and Wanda's taped voice, clipped and businesslike, advising the caller to leave a message at the sound of the tone.

Penny ignored it, concentrating on putting the *Mc*s and *Mac*s in their proper alphabetical sequence in the card file. They were abominably mixed up.

"I always feel like such a damned fool talking to one of these machines," someone said. "I'll catch you later."

Recognizing the voice that had caused her so much trouble, Penny leapt up and nearly knocked the wastebasket over getting to the phone.

"Mr. Wheeler?" she cried, snatching up the receiver.

He didn't answer at first, and she thought he'd hung up. "Is this a real live human being on the line?"

"Yes. Oh, I'm so glad to hear from you."

He snorted. "This sure as hell can't be Wanda then."

"We spoke briefly on the telephone yesterday. Mr. Korda is most anxious to speak with you."

"Then put him on, sweetheart."

"He isn't in the office."

"I can't very well talk to him then, can I?" he said, chuckling.

What should she do? Steffan hadn't even left a number where he could be reached. But Wanda might know. "Can I call you back when I locate him?"

"'Fraid not, honey. I'm on my way out the door. Tell the big man I'll try and drop by the beginning of the week."

"Oh, please wait a few minutes, and—"

"Chewed you out about not getting my call, did he?"

"He was somewhat upset."

"Korda was born upset. How can you stand working for him? Hell, I don't like to make trouble for you. Tell you what—will he be there later tonight?"

"I'm sure he will be." Penny wasn't sure. But she'd track him down by then, whatever it took. "Can you call back?"

"Nope. Sonny Wheeler's hard-and-fast rule for avoiding ulcers is no business after hours."

"Then...?"

"What do you say I pick you up, we have a nice candlelight dinner somewhere and get to know each other? For you, I'll bend my rule slightly. If Korda happens to be there, I'll give him five minutes before we go."

Penny, who'd snatched up a pen to jot down his number, began to scribble in her frustration—daggers and dollar signs. "I don't think so," she said.

"Why not? You married?"

"No. But I have a rule of my own. I don't go out with men I don't know."

"I can respect that. But it puts us at a standoff, doesn't ·it? Hold on a minute, cutie." He said something to someone in the background. It was muffled, and Penny could tell he'd put his hand over the receiver. Then he was back to Penny. "Okay. Tell Korda we'll aim for a conversation on Monday or Tuesday, if I make it back. I'll be flying out in the morning. It was nice talking to you."

"Wait." Penny dropped the pencil and clutched the receiver with both hands. When she and Steffan were out with the Laceys and she'd argued that Verna was rude and insulting, Steffan had said, "I don't give a damn if she's Lucretia Borgia. Do your job." Annoying as he was, Sonny Wheeler was important to one of Steffan's business deals, and getting them together was part of her job.

"Change your mind?" Sonny asked slyly, knowing she had.

"Yes."

"Does eight o'clock sound right to you?"

She squeezed her eyes shut. "Yes. Eight o'clock sounds fine."

"Where will I pick you up?"

"Here, at the Korda villa. I'm in the white guest cottage."

"Right. See you then, sweetheart."

A tap behind her made her turn as she hung up. "Knock, knock," Wanda trilled, as if she'd just arrived, though Penny would have bet she'd been standing there for some time. "I just stopped by to see if everything's okay."

"It is, I suppose."

"You don't sound too sure." The woman outlined the edge of the light switch with one finger, stalling. "Isn't dating Sonny Wheeler above and beyond the call of duty?"

So she had been listening. "It's not really a date," Penny assured her.

"Using Sonny to make Steffan jealous might not be such a good idea. Those two aren't the best of friends, you know. I always expect them to come to blows when they meet."

"These are special circumstances. And this is strictly business. Steffan would approve."

"Because of the Wayfarer acquisition, you mean?"

"Yes." As she moved around the office, straightening her desk, putting chairs in place and trying to make everything look as orderly as it had when she'd arrived that morning, Penny explained about Sonny's call. About how he was flying out of town, and how she'd had to make the date to ensure that he and Steffan got together first.

"Oh, kid," Wanda groaned. "I wish you'd checked with me. Steffan won't be here tonight. He and your pa have driven off to parts unknown and won't be back until early tomorrow morning. Lon left you a note."

"Another of his infamous notes?" Penny snapped. "There must be a number where they can be reached. Something. Doesn't Steffan have a beeper?"

"Yes, but he isn't using it. You know how hush-hush everything is when your father's—"

"When he's playing Captain Kidd and arranging details for his treasure-hunting nonsense," Penny said, finishing Wanda's sentence for her. "Wonderful. So Steffan's on a wild-goose chase, and I'm stuck with Sonny Boy Wheeler because no one wanted to tell me what's going on." But Wanda had been told, hadn't she? Penny couldn't help thinking. It always came down to that. Steffan, Lon and Wanda on one side. Penny on the other.

"It isn't all that bad." Wanda leaned against the door frame and crossed her arms in front of her. "Sonny's reasonably good-looking, if you like the type, and he's a big spender. You'll go somewhere fabulous and may even end up having a good time.''

"Are you serious?"

"I'm just trying to look on the bright side." The woman shrugged. "Let me know how it comes out."

CHAPTER ELEVEN

"WHAT NOW?" Penny groaned.

She had just managed to get her bath water to the perfect temperature. She'd poured in her favorite perfumed oil and settled into the tub, when there were three sharp raps on the front door.

Was it Wanda again? If she simply ignored the knocking, the woman might go away. Or did she have a key? Probably. Penny didn't want to be rude, but she didn't feel like her company, either. When the raps came again, louder this time, she got out and wrapped herself in her father's terry bathrobe. Muttering to herself, dripping water, she trekked to the front door.

Her visitor filled the eye and the doorway. If she hadn't known better, she would have thought he was in full football-player's gear. His sandy hair was cut short and worn flat to his head. His face was round, pink and cherubic, and he was wearing an ear-to-ear grin.

"Please tell me you're Penelope," he pleaded.

"I'm Penelope," she said obediently. "And you're Garrett Wheeler?"

"Sonny," he said.

Gathering the robe more closely about her, she peered at the clock. "You're almost an hour early. I've just begun to get ready."

"I was in the neighborhood." He gestured widely. "Take your time. I don't mind waiting. As long as it's inside."

He brushed past her to the couch and settled there with his huge feet propped on the coffee table.

"I'm afraid you've made the trip for nothing," she told him, smoothing her hair back from her forehead. "I wasn't able to reach Steffan. So if you'd like to make it another time..."

"It wasn't Korda who brought me here tonight, sweetheart. I've got a thing about voices, and I'm usually right on the money when it comes to judging who's behind them. This time is no exception. I lucked out." He raised his eyebrows three quick times in succession. "That sly dog. Got you living right on the premises, has he?"

Penny pressed her lips together, wondering how she'd ever get through the evening. "I only arrived from St. Louis a few days ago. Steffan was kind enough to allow us the use of this cottage until we're able to find a place of our own."

That sobered him. "Us?"

"My father and I."

He took his feet off the coffee table and looked over his shoulder. "Uh... am I going to have the, uh, pleasure of meeting him? Your father, that is?"

"No, he isn't here," she said, then noticing the gleam that came into his pale gray eyes, added quickly, "but I expect him at any time."

He got up and walked around the room, drawing a hand over the mantelpiece and studying the candlesticks as if he were a used-furniture dealer. "It's real cozy back here now, with the walls painted white. Doesn't look so much like a dungeon."

"You've been here before?"

He picked up a glass unicorn, tossed it from one hand to the other, and held it up to the light before putting it down again. "A while back." He bent down to read the titles of the books in the bookcase. "You can learn a hell of a lot more about a gal by spending five minutes in her place than you can by talking to her for five hours."

"That's an interesting theory."

"It's a fact. Now you're a puzzle. You say you haven't been here long, but it's my experience that women put their signature on a room right off. And what have we got here? No *House Beautiful*. No *Glamour*. Not even a supermarket tabloid.'' He picked up a folder Lon had left on the side table, flipped through the pages and found the treasure map. He chuckled, shaking his head. "You're a gal with peculiar interests.''

She fluttered one hand. "Those things belong to my father,'' she said, wondering why Lon, who was so secretive about his ventures, would have left the information lying out in the open. Of course, he hadn't expected any visitors.

"That makes more sense.'' Sonny ran a finger along the red arrows. "X marks the spot, hey? Is this where he thinks it'll happen for him?''

Penny took the folder, closed it and stuck it in the top drawer of the desk. "At the moment. But this is only the latest map in a dozen—maybe a hundred. He was almost killed not long ago, chasing his impossible dreams. Anyone else would have—'' She stopped abruptly. Why was she raving on to a virtual stranger? "I'd better get dressed, if you still want to go out to dinner.''

"You bet. Wait!'' Sonny guffawed and slapped a hand to his thigh. "You're Alonzo Haywood's daughter. Hell, I should have known. You're the spitting image of him.'' He came toward her, grinning. "Be tolerant, honey. Everybody's gotta have a dream, like the song says.''

"I'm not against dreaming, Mr. Wheeler,'' she assured him, irritated at hearing the same old argument. "I'm only against it when—''

"Cool it, sweetheart.'' He raised his hands in surrender. "I'm not a fighter. And the name is Sonny, remember?''

"I find it difficult to call you that.''

"You don't think it fits? Let me explain. I was the only boy in a family of five girls, all of whom arrived on the scene before I did. My father was worried that there'd be no male to carry on the family name.''

"Horror of horrors.''

"Naturally, when I appeared, I was spoiled rotten.''

"Naturally."

"Mom used to say I was her sunshine. Kids in the neighborhood heard her say that unfortunately, and I was called Sunshine for years. You'll never know how many fights that nickname caused me. Then it was shortened to Sonny, and I got used to it."

As she dressed, he played records, hummed to himself, and now and then stood at the closed bedroom door to relate a tale he thought hilarious about some of the uptight, too-serious types he did business with.

"What's it all about?" he wanted to know. "If they don't know how to enjoy life?"

What was the problem between him and Steffan? Penny couldn't help wondering. Was it true that they hated each other? If so, why?

He wasn't so terrible. He had a good sense of humor and an easy manner. At least he wasn't the obnoxious oaf she'd expected. She might even like him if he'd stop calling her sweetheart and honey and cookie....

Wanda had been right about his taking her to a fabulous restaurant. The atmosphere was elegant, the seafood dinner delectable, and the floor show, a magician with a lineup of attractive assistants in breathtaking costumes, spectacular. Sonny was courteous, interested in her opinions, and most surprising of all, kept his hands to himself.

The evening might not turn out to be such a catastrophe after all, she mused. Steffan had promised he wouldn't let her father get hurt; so perhaps he was using their trip together to help her father see the futility of his ways. And now *she* had Sonny Wheeler in her clutches and wouldn't let him out of her sight until he promised to get in touch with Steffan as soon as possible.

"I don't suppose you'd like to make me a cup of coffee for the road," Sonny asked, as he walked Penny to her door.

"Coffee at this hour will interfere with your sleep."

"Not mine," he assured her. "I always sleep like a baby. Probably because I have a clear conscience."

She smiled at his impish little-boy grin. "Probably."

When they were inside, she filled the coffeepot and set out cups and saucers while Sonny shuffled through the stack of records in the stereo cabinet. "Why is it so difficult to get in touch with you?" she asked. "Don't you live in Athens?"

"Yep. But I change my residence as often as I change my socks. And to allow for uninterrupted enjoyment of life, I frequently unplug the telephone."

"Then why on earth have one?"

"A damned good question."

"Don't you have an office?"

"Only my slaves turn up there. It's a horrible place. Typewriters clacking away. Computers lighting up. Ugh."

His mention of slaves brought her own job to mind. "I'd appreciate it if I could count on you to give Steffan a call in the morning before you fly out."

"Fly out?"

"Yes. You told me—"

"Uh-oh." He brought his hands to his face and looked at her through his twined fingers. "I have a confession. No, two confessions."

"What are they?" Penny waited, fairly certain she wasn't going to like what he would tell her.

"One, Korda and I already got together and came to an agreement. Two, I'm not flying anywhere. Matter of fact, I'm throwing a party Friday night and you're invited."

"You said . . ." Penny sputtered. "When did—"

"I told you I was skippng town or you never would have agreed to tonight." Pleased with himself, he picked up one of the records he'd been looking through and brought it closer to his eyes to read the title. "As to when this historic meeting took place, it was last night. Korda smoked me out at a little café in Syntagma Square. That's when I got curious about you, too."

"About me? Why?"

"I asked about the new girl in the office. Just trying to be friendly, you know? He cut me off just like that." Sonny snapped his fingers. "Got even more uptight than usual. So I figured you'd be a little beauty he wanted to keep for himself. Turns out I was right."

Penny shut off the flame under the pot. No coffee for him. "I don't like tricks."

"I know. But I didn't have to tell you. And it's been fun up to now, hasn't it? Forgive me?" Before she could reply, he'd dropped the record, closed the gap between them and wound his incredibly long arms around her like a giant squid. "Let's kiss and make it better, sweetheart."

Her struggles only encouraged him, and before she could react, he'd swung her off her feet and was maneuvering her to the couch. "Let's cut the kid games. We're both adults here, with adult needs."

His line infuriated her even more, and she shoved him hard. Scrambling to her feet, she put the coffee table between them. An umbrella in the stand next to the window caught her eye, and she snatched it up, swinging it into batting position.

"Good night, Mr. Wheeler."

"Sonny," he corrected her, out of habit, breathing hard. Big as he was, he was out of condition.

"Time to go home, *Mister* Wheeler," she said.

"Aw, don't be like that, sweetheart," he tried, using a stomach-turning, mush-mouthed voice that was supposed to melt her determination. "Do you know what you do to me?"

"My father will be home any minute."

He drew back. "Why the righteous act? You knew what to expect when you invited me in."

"I expected you to behave like a gentleman."

He stood perfectly still, trying to decide what to do. "Your old man isn't coming home, cookie," he sneered. "He's in the sack with Wanda. You think you're cramping their style by staying here? Hell, her pad is a two-minute drive away. You could throw a rock and hit it."

"Get out!"

"Who are you saving yourself for? The Big Man? Korda? Forget it. You haven't got a prayer." His laugh was ugly and menacing as he hurled himself out the front door, slamming it behind him.

Usually Penny was able to rise above such things, considering the source. The whole episode—her wrestling match with Sonny and having to fend him off with an umbrella—was funny, wasn't it, now that it was over?

But his vicious remarks stayed with her through the night and remained in the morning. Unable to keep her eyes closed any longer, she got up early. After a halfhearted breakfast she sat in the small enclosed garden outside the kitchen window with her sketch pad, hoping to come up with something special for Sun Dial before she had to go into the office.

"Dare to Dazzle," she scribbled tentatively under the drawing of the smiling woman in a flowery Sun Dial suit.

No, it wasn't right.

The scent of flowers distracted her, and she set her work on the bench. No need to rush. She had more than a week before her next meeting with Alex. Plenty of time to coax the right look out of the shadowy corners of her mind. Her best ideas always came when she didn't try too hard. She decided to gather a fragrant bouquet to cheer herself up and returned to the kitchen for a pair of scissors.

Methodically, she began selecting roses in vibrant shades of red and pink, with white ones for contrast. She jumped when she heard footsteps and saw Steffan coming down the garden path toward her, sticking her finger on a thorn. Despite the pain, a flush of pleasure washed over her, as it always did at the sight of him. He was dressed casually, the way she liked him best, in a shirt the color of vanilla ice cream, trim brown slacks and well-shined but worn loafers. If he was still upset with her, it didn't show.

"You haven't got a prayer," Sonny had thrown at her. He had been trying to be mean, but there was a chunk of truth in his words. Steffan had warned her that she could never be more to him than Lon's daughter. She'd be wise to keep that fact front and center at all times.

"Now what did I do?" she asked as he approached, bringing the injured finger to her mouth. "It must be serious for you to come back here after me."

He took one of the roses she had cut and held it to his nose. "Do you always think the worst?"

"Lately, yes." She wondered if he'd laugh if she told him of her experience with Sonny the night before. She decided he wouldn't.

"I'm sorry about the way I lit into you yesterday about Wheeler's phone call."

"I deserved it."

"It's just that I'd waited so long to get Wheeler to agree to this deal."

"You don't have to explain."

"It will put a finish on what has long been unfinished business. It'll put the past behind and make me feel that any achievements from here on are my own."

"I understand." Steffan's acquisition of this particular hotel wasn't something he needed to prove his worth to his father, as she had first suspected. It was something that would allow him to prove that worth to himself.

"Would you like to take a long drive? This is a good day for it, if you don't mind mixing business with pleasure."

"When? Now?" It was early. Almost half an hour before she'd expected to go to work.

"Yes, I'd like an early start. There are some papers Yuri Stravos has to sign. You can be our witness and have a wonderful dinner at the same time. His wife, Marissa, is a spectacular cook."

Yuri Stravos. Penny recognized his name as being one of the Big Three Wanda had talked about. Now that Sonny had agreed to the sale, Yuri's signature would put the Wayfarer entirely in Steffan's hands.

"It'll take the whole day," he said. "If you don't want to go, I'll understand."

"I'd love to," she said, eager for the chance to share his joy. "But I'd better change." The rust-colored shirt and dark brown pants were fine for the office, but not smart enough for a business trip, not even with the addition of a double strand of chocolate and ivory beads.

"You're fine as you are," he said with a careless gesture. "I'd take Wanda, but she has other plans for the day and I don't want to disrupt them. Besides, you can use some time away from the grind."

Thanks, Steffan, she said to herself, working to prevent a telltale expression of disappointment. *Remind me where I stand. Hit me over the head with it, just in case I might think you asked me along because you really want my company.*

Sunlight through the tree branches made a pattern on his face, touched his eyes with gold and banished her resentment. She used to feel giddy when she looked at him ten years ago, and she felt that way now. Would it be the same in another ten years? In twenty? Would the simple act of standing and talking with any other man ever affect her so?

"More swimsuits?" He picked up her sketch pad and studied it. "'Dare to Dazzle,'" he read aloud.

"It's part of an advertising campaign."

"Oh?" He frowned and turned the page. "'Celebrate Summer in a Sun Dial Suit.' You're very talented."

"Thank you." She shrugged off his compliment. "I'm doing some free-lance work for Sun Dial."

He turned another page and nodded. "You're working for this fellow I saw you with at Bretannia's?"

"Yes."

"I see." His smile was a shallow one that barely touched his lips. "It seems I don't keep you busy enough."

"I enjoy this kind of work, and the extra money will come in handy." She didn't have to add that it would go toward settling her debt to him. The explanation seemed to hang in the air between them.

"We should go now," he said tightly. "If you're ready."

"I'll get my bag."

"Get a wrap, too, and do whatever else you have to do. I'll meet you in front of the house in, say, fifteen minutes."

The road that led to Corinth was a wide, well-traveled one that afforded little of exceptional interest beyond the varying shades of green in the surrounding hills and the brilliant blue sky of a typical Grecian summer day. Like most roads here, it wound through country rich in lore and legend. But Steffan, Penny knew, wasn't thinking about the Temple of Apollo or the headless lions guarding Agamemnon's Palace today. Soon the Wayfarer would be his, and he could talk of nothing else.

Off the highway and over a wooden bridge, they took a road that led through a stand of eucalyptus trees and brought them before the door of a sprawling old house of glistening white, surrounded by banks of geraniums in every imaginable color.

They were greeted by Yuri himself, a stocky man, with a mane of bristly white hair and a crushing handshake. He ushered them loudly to a huge kitchen, where his wife, Marissa, served them a delicious meal of steaming vegetable soup and homemade bread.

"You're looking good," Yuri told Steffan, gesturing with a chunk of bread. "Doesn't he look good?"

"He's a handsome boy," Marissa agreed.

"Has she got something to do with it?" He jerked his head toward Penny and winked.

Marissa laid a fragile hand on her husband's arm. "None of your teasing now. You'll embarrass these young people."

"Embarrass, hell," he growled. "Young people don't embarrass these days. Tell me, Penelope. How long have you known this guy?"

"That's difficult to answer," Penny said. "I've known him since I was six. We were next-door neighbors. But I've only been working for him for a few days."

"You got her working for you?" Yuri bellowed, dunking his bread into his soup. "You lucky son-of-a-gun. You should see my secretary. She could turn the Medusa into stone."

"I hired her," Marissa said. "She's a good secretary."

"But not entirely pleasant to face in the morning. Which may be why I'm retiring."

Marissa was as petite and soft-spoken as her husband was big and explosive. The two complemented each other perfectly, Penny thought, instantly liking them both. The deep love they shared was obvious from the way they looked at each other, belying the playful bickering they exchanged throughout the meal.

After dinner, Steffan and Yuri sat down to discuss business over strong cups of coffee. Marissa and Penny cleared the table and stacked the dishwasher. Then Marissa went to her room to change the blouse she'd spattered during the cleanup, and Penny went out to the car to get her purse so that she could repair her lipstick.

When the white convertible approached, she shaded her eyes against the sun. The driver's shirt was such a startling splash of color, it caught her attention before the round pink face and the Cheshire Cat grin.

Sonny. She hadn't realized it was necessary for him to be here to finalize the deal. She pressed her lips together, hoping his resentment over the events of the night before wouldn't make him abusive.

When he'd nosed the car into position a few inches from her, he hiked himself up and swung out of it without opening the door, reminding her of a sixth-grader showing off for the new girl at school.

"Penelope, sweetheart," he drawled. "If I'd known you were going to be here, I'd have made it a point to arrive on time."

"Too bad you didn't."

"Aw, you missed me."

"No, but you missed a delicious meal."

"Marissa's famous soup." He held one hand to his stomach and grimaced. "That soup is why I'm late, cutie. I'm a meat-and-potatoes man, myself. Can't you tell by looking at me?"

"I'm afraid not."

When she started back toward the house, he reached out and caught her arm. His thumb moved in insinuating circles on her skin. "Hey. I want to remind you about my party Friday night. It's at the Hotel Markham. Suite fourteen sixty-eight."

She wrenched herself free and smoothed her fingers along her arm where his hand had been. "Like the party we had last night?"

"So I made a mistake. You can't blame a guy for trying."

"Actually, I can."

"But you have a forgiving nature." He dropped his chin against his chest and tried to look contrite. "Tell me if I'm wrong."

"You're wrong."

"Friday night. Suite fourteen sixty-eight," he repeated, leaning toward her so that his forehead almost touched hers. "I know you have to be cool about it. Korda's the boss and all, and in his book I'm Beelzebub himself."

"Sorry. I'll be busy Friday night."

"Doing what?"

"I don't know. I'll think of something. Shall we go in now? The others are waiting."

"I'll just bet they're waiting." His grin broke into a chuckle. "Bet Korda's worn out the floor pacing. Afraid I'll change my mind."

So that was why Steffan had been so nervous and kept looking at the clock. Undoubtedly that was why Sonny had come late, too. To taunt him.

"Actually he seems very relaxed," Penny lied. "It's good to get away from the city and spend some time with friends. Yuri and Marissa are terribly nice people, aren't they?"

He hunched his shoulders. "But not exactly a laugh a minute, hey?"

"Penny!" Steffan's voice was so sharp it startled her, and she gasped at the sound. "Marissa has been looking for you." His deep-set eyes were shadowed by the arched entranceway, making them look hollow. His jaw looked exaggeratedly square, making a caricature of his face.

"I came out to get my purse," she said.

He looked pointedly at her empty hands. "And did you get it?"

"No...I—"

"It's my fault," Sonny said, with a show of gallantry that somehow sounded incriminating. "I didn't know she was on duty." He laid a solicitous hand on Penny's shoulder and gazed into her eyes. "Want me to get it for you, sweetheart?"

"No, thank you."

"Can we carry on with business then?" Steffan snarled. "That's what we came here for, isn't it?"

Fortunately Marissa met them at the door and invited Penny to see her collection of fans, so she was spared the need to go into the library with the men. Sonny would take advantage of the opportunity to bedevil Steffan, and might well have used her to do it.

Marissa had an array of fans that should have been in a museum. Made of dozens of different materials, they had been gathered from all parts of the world. Some had belonged to peasants and some to poets. Some had been used by presidents' wives and some by kings' mistresses.

Yuri's voice, though the men were several rooms away, carried through most of the house. Penny wasn't trying to listen, but she could hear most of what he was saying. She heard him telling Sonny goodbye and advising him to watch the twists in the road back to the highway. She heard him bellow that he was glad business was over and could be forgotten. It was time for a drink to celebrate. Then she could hear words of annoyance directed at Steffan. Yuri, it seemed, had planned for the two of them to drive to Naplio that evening. There was someone he wanted Steffan to meet.

"Why the hell can't you? How often do I ask a favor, eh? So you stay over and drive back in the morning. The girls will have a good time without us underfoot."

"I have to get Penny home," Steffan insisted.

"Is she Cinderella, that one?"

"It's all right, Steffan," Penny said, coming back to the library grateful that Sonny had departed without incident. "I can call my father and let him know we're staying. If he isn't there, someone at the house will surely get a message to him."

"You're sure?" Steffan frowned.

"Yes, she's sure," Marissa said, hurrying over to give Penny a hug. "It's been so long since we had a houseguest, and I have so many things to show her."

A tour of the house began when the men had driven away. The aura of years past existed not only inside, but in the garden, as well. Vines hung tenaciously to the entire north wall, almost obscuring it. Greenery, lush and thick, was allowed to grow whichever way it would, with little human interference.

"I apologize for Yuri's teasing," Marissa remarked as they passed under an arched trellis and into a circular clearing walled in by miniature roses. "He likes you. He didn't mean anything. I hope you didn't take offense."

"How could I?"

"We're very fond of Steffan, you know. I can tell you are, too." She raised a hand to stop Penny's protest. "I think you'd make him very happy. I have a feeling about such things."

"But I only work for him."

"I used to work for Yuri, too."

"We don't even get along very well."

"You should be here when Yuri and I have one of our spats. The fur fairly flies. That's all part of it you know—and the part that makes the rest better."

Penny had to smile at the woman's idea. It revolved around a ridiculous cliché that had never been true as far as she was concerned. No relationship was better after a bitter quarrel. "The making up, you mean?"

"Ah, yes. The making up." The woman's face colored, and she looked over Penny's shoulder at nothing in particular, remembering. "Anyway," she said finally. "It's time Steffan settled down. He isn't getting any younger. But he's been hurt, you know. Hurt badly."

"By his mother's desertion, you mean."

Marissa pursed her lips and nodded. "That, yes. And, well, you knew he was engaged to be married about three years ago, didn't you? She was a lovely girl. Tall and willowy, with perfect cheekbones and great dark eyes."

"I didn't know," Penny said quietly.

"Perhaps I shouldn't have said anything."

"What happened between them?"

"He found her with another man and that was the end of it. There were no second chances. He's a Capricorn, you know. As with most children of Saturn, he can be unforgiving."

Marissa said nothing more on the subject, and of course, Penny couldn't ask. But it wasn't easy for her to drive away the picture of Steffan and the tall, willowy girl with perfect cheekbones and great dark eyes. He had loved her enough to ask her to be his wife.

Though she couldn't help feeling jealousy, an even stronger feeling was her sympathy for Steffan and the pain he must have suffered over this ill-fated love affair.

Who was the girl? Where was she? Did he still love her? Did he see her when he looked at other women? Did he see her when he looked at Penny?

When they went inside again, Marissa showed her a breathtaking collection of quilts she'd made over the years. The one she was working on now was a "Bride's Quilt." It was entirely white, with impossibly small stitches that created an elaborate pattern of birds and flowers.

Then, over cups of herb tea and thin slices of fruit-filled bread, the woman, eyes bright with building excitement, talked about old houses and the ghosts they invariably contained.

"We have one of our own," she boasted proudly. "A lovely young girl."

"You've seen her?" Penny asked politely. People who wanted to see ghosts usually managed to persuade themselves that they had. And there was no harm in it.

"Glimpses, no more. Her flowing dress as she rounds a corner. The glow of a candle. But I hear her footsteps sometimes at night, and her voice singing some sad love song that makes me want to cry."

At ten o'clock Marissa was ready to retire, and she showed Penny to the room that would be hers. It was small but charming, with a high four-poster, a padded window seat and ruffled sheer curtains. The room had been furnished, the woman said, by her great-grandmother. Only the bedding, the curtains and a tall glass cabinet, which held dozens of dolls, had been added since.

"This was my room," she explained, "and these dolls were my friends. I talked to them and imagined they were answering. You see, there weren't any children for me to play with—it's so remote here—and the dolls helped keep me from missing the companionship."

She opened the bottom drawer of the dresser. "You'll find some nightdresses in here. One of them will fit, I'm sure. Oh, and please remember, we leave a light burning in the bathroom at the end of the hall. Good night, my dear. If you feel restless, as most of us do when we're sleeping in a strange house, don't hesitate to patter out to the kitchen for a snack. I'm not a light sleeper."

As Penny bathed in the old-fashioned claw-footed tub, inhaled the fragrance of the lavender-scented bath soap she'd used and slipped into a white bastiste nightgown, she began to feel as if she were part of a world long past.

When she crawled into the too-soft bed to confront the crowded shelves of doll faces, she found she wasn't at all comforted by them. The staring glass eyes, all seemingly fixed on her, were disquieting, lit as they were by the moonlight streaming through the window. She had to force her eyes to close and her mind to concentrate on sleep.

She awoke to a thump and a creaking that seemed to originate inside the wall behind her head. Marissa's ghost, she thought wryly. She sat upright and listened. But the sounds she'd heard must have existed only in her dreams. They'd done the trick, though. She was wide-awake and her mouth was dry. Visions of the marvelous fruit bread she'd shared with her hostess sprang into her head, and she thought how good a slice would taste with another cup of herb tea.

For at least half an hour she lingered over her snack, thumbing through some decade-old magazines and trying not to think about the futility of loving Steffan, until her eyelids felt heavy.

It seemed much darker in the hallway after the brightness of the kitchen, and she had to feel her way slowly, not wanting to make any noise. Her hand fumbled for the glass knob, which she turned to let herself back into her room.

The room seemed darker, too. As she was about to crawl into bed, a realization struck her and she froze. The curtains had been open before, she was certain. Now they were closed. The moonlight only filtered now through the gauzy fabric. A shiver swept through her. The creaking had begun again—in the hallway—and the door inched open. She pressed a fist to her mouth and stopped breathing.

It was Steffan. He wore a short bathrobe, and a towel was draped over one shoulder. His feet were bare, and his hair was damp from the shower.

"Penny," he whispered.

"I . . . I couldn't sleep," she said.

An unnerving silence fell between them as she wondered at his coming to her this way. She would never have expected it of him, and yet she was so overjoyed she wanted to hurl herself into his arms and cover his face with kisses. She wouldn't. The move had to be his. Her pulses began to pound.

"The shower doesn't work," he told her, picking up the ragged thread of their conversation. "It makes a horrendous racket."

"I didn't notice. I took a bath."

"Did you? It's what I ended up doing. Did the sound of the pipes wake you?"

She said no, though realized they probably had. All she knew now was that her lips ached with a need for his. A fiery warmth whirred through her.

He smiled crookedly. "You gave me a start. When I saw you standing in the shadows in that long flowing gown, I thought you were Marissa's ghost."

"She's told you about her, too?"

"It's by far her favorite subject. And you almost made a believer out of me."

Penny tried to match his smile, but couldn't. "You may think this is foolish, but it was the dolls that bothered me. When I tried to sleep, I could feel all those pairs of eyes on me, staring." She looked at the wall opposite the bed, looked away, then jerked her head back again. There were no dolls. There was no cabinet. The bed wasn't even a fourposter. She swallowed hard. Steffan hadn't come to her room. She had inadvertently walked into his. Her face flamed.

He moved slowly toward her, grazed her cheek with his hand and allowed it to come to rest at the back of her neck. All of her sensations rushed to the place his fingers played. "You're very likely a ghost, after all. The way you've been haunting me."

"I'm . . . sorry," she stammered.

"What are you sorry for?" he asked. "You're wonderful. More wonderful than I deserve. Your openness and honesty, despite everything I've said and done, overwhelms me."

He lowered his mouth to gently touch each of her eyelids in turn, then gathered her to him. She nestled there, feeling that she belonged, her eyes still closed by his kisses as she breathed in the heady scent that was only his. His robe felt vaguely rough against her cheek, but she didn't care.

She was honest, he had said. She had to tell him that her being in his room now was a mistake. Hadn't he warned her that his feelings were fleeting physical ones that would vanish when they were appeased? He assumed she had come to him anyway, accepting his terms.

"Thank God one of us is sane," he murmured, nudging her away only enough to allow his feverish lips access to hers. Moving his head back and forth, he kissed her ravenously until her reason had flown. Her head fell back, and his breath caressed her throat.

Perhaps she really hadn't awakened at all, she thought dreamily. Maybe she hadn't gone to the kitchen at all. Maybe she wasn't with Steffan now. Never had she felt anything so wonderful when she was awake. She kept her eyes tightly closed, just in case, needing to hold on to what she was experiencing as long as possible.

Now his hands were at the hollow of her waist, now they were moving along her arms, and now at her sides. The thoroughness of his investigation was too much for the ill-fitting borrowed garment. The too-wide shoulders were displaced, slipped down and bared one of her breasts. Steffan's eager mouth made the discovery much too quickly for her to react, and closed over it, creating such havoc inside her that her modesty was entirely defeated.

"There's enough room in that gown for both of us," he whispered, then added, "an idea rich in possibilities."

Her answer was a shuddering sigh.

"Are you cold?" he asked.

"I don't know." How could she give a name to what she was feeling?

"I'll warm you," he promised with renewed urgency, imprisoning her so tightly that the thin fabric of her nightdress offered no barrier at all against the consuming flames of their shared passion.

Soon she would be over the edge. It would happen between them; there would be nothing to stop it. But her soaring spirit demanded more. She couldn't surrender herself so completely unless she knew that what happened between them happened in Steffan's heart and mind, as well as his body.

"I . . . I thought this was my room," she heard herself saying from somewhere far off. "It was so dark, I took the wrong door coming from the kitchen."

He placed a kiss at one corner of her mouth, then the other, and she felt relieved. He hadn't heard her confession. Let him believe what he wanted to believe.

But his next kiss was less certain, and he pulled back. "I might have known," he muttered.

"I'm sorry."

"Don't apologize," he snapped, then immediately took her face between his hands. "I really am a fool. I have no business jumping on you."

"I wish I had come to your room," she whispered. "Deliberately, I mean."

A corner of his mouth lifted. "Then it's just as if you did."

Someone coughed in another room, much closer than either of them had realized, and their eyes touched with a jolt.

"We should say good-night," Penny said. "Yuri and Marissa . . ."

"Not to mention the ghost."

"I didn't mean . . ." she began, stretching out her arms to him as she rethought her refusal.

"Yes, you did, and you're right. You'd better go while I'm still able to stick to my convictions. We have to get up in the morning. It's a working day, and I understand your boss is a tyrant."

"He is. But I know how to handle him."

"That you do." He tilted her chin for a final kiss, then walked her to the door. "It doesn't end here, Sparrow," he said. "There's tomorrow."

And tomorrow and tomorrow and tomorrow, she thought, as she closed herself into her own room.

CHAPTER TWELVE

"WE'VE BEEN TOGETHER record time without doing battle," Steffan remarked as they turned into the tree-lined drive that led to the Korda villa. "You're being much too agreeable. Should I watch my step?"

"Maybe you should," Penny said. "And you're being entirely too considerate. Should I guess you have an ulterior motive?"

"You can bank on it," he said, bringing the car to a stop inside the garage. "And you'll discover what it is when the time is right."

The drive home had been perfect. Steffan had related amusing highlights of the evening spent with Yuri and his friends in a crowded café, and Penny had talked about Marissa's lovely garden and exquisite quilts. But for most of the ride, they sat in companionable silence.

They didn't make any stops to see the sights. They would see them together soon, he told her, and he wanted everything to be new and fresh. They'd come back and explore the pebbly villages on foot, the sandy bays, the rocky slopes and the forests of feathery pine.

"When the time is right," she repeated, teasing. Was Steffan so firmly entrenched in the business world that even love had to run on a timetable? "Why isn't the time right? The Wayfarer is yours now."

"I'm not talking about that," he said. "I mean the arrangement with Nikko Minotis. The diving, the search. The truth about exactly what is or isn't in those waters off Naxos."

Still halfway into a kind of carefree reverie, it took Penny a moment or two to realize what he was saying. "But there won't be any search, will there? How can there be if you aren't supplying the money?"

Steffan's eyes darkened. "I told you. I'm giving Lon whatever he needs."

"You can't do that. You promised." The real world sprang into focus. She felt betrayed.

"I promised only that Lon wouldn't be hurt. I intend to be there every step of the way to keep that promise. The funny thing about all this is that Yuri's intrigued by the story, too, and wants in."

"You're not serious."

"Why not? It's a fascinating tale."

"A tale is all it is. Surely Marissa will put her foot down."

"Marissa will go along with whatever makes her husband happy, as long as there isn't any danger. And there's no reason to believe there will be."

"There never is," she said bitterly, reaching for the door handle.

Steffan caught her hand gently and brought it to his lips. "We're running down next week. To the islands, I mean. We're going to settle the financial details with Nikko, map out a plan and see about a crew. Why don't you come along? Your vote of confidence will mean a lot to Lon."

Unshed tears burned in her eyes. "Last night meant nothing to you."

"It meant everything. But the one hasn't got a damn thing to do with the other. We have an arrangement, he and I. One last time. Then he's agreed to slow down. To go about his treasure hunting on a part-time basis."

"You believe that?"

"I have no reason to doubt it."

"I have. A hundred reasons to go with a hundred broken promises."

"I think he means it this time. He's no fool. He was shaken by what happened in Peru, even if he won't admit it.

And when you get right down to it, the prospect of uncovering enough wealth to allow him to light his cigars with hundred-dollar bills isn't what drives him.''

"What is it then?"

"It's the pursuit itself, not the treasure. It's the dream, the excitement of making plans and the anticipation of what could be. He can still have all that even if he does slow down. And Wanda's pretty sure she can convince him to write a book about his experiences."

"A book? My father?"

"Why not? He's got some fascinating stories to tell, and his know-how could be a big help to would-be salvagers."

"Do you really believe what you're saying? Do you?"

"Penny—"

"You knew how much this meant to me, and still you chose to go ahead with it." She slapped away the hand that held hers, opened the car door and let herself out. "Stay away from me," she cried.

The old anger blazed in his eyes as he sprang out, too, and strode after her to cut off her escape. Strong fingers curled around her wrist and squeezed. "Don't ever pull away from me again, Penny. We're people with strong feelings, you and I. We'll have a lifetime of disagreements. Call me names. Kick, stamp your feet, throw things. But don't pull away."

With a thrust of his free hand, he caught her about the waist and yanked her to him. The hand that was at her wrist moved to the back of her head, to tangle there and hold her steady for a feverish, shattering kiss. It was a kiss that would have left her numb and speechless, if she hadn't been so filled with rock-hard determination.

His lips fell desperately on hers, pleading and demanding at the same time, but when he released her, she stood perfectly still, piercing his eyes with her own. "It worked for you before," she said, steeling herself against him. "But don't expect it to work for you again."

Hurt flashed across his face. "What the hell are you talking about?"

"About you. Pretending to care."

He cursed under his breath. "When we disagree, will you always expect me to give in?"

"Only when I'm right," she whispered savagely.

"And who decides if you're right? Like it or not, I care for your father as much as you do. Maybe more, because I'm determined to leave him with some of his pride."

"Pride," she groaned, twisting away again. This time when she ran, he didn't call after her or try to follow.

"Good movie on the tube," her father drawled as she burst in. "*High Noon.* Gary Cooper, Grace Kelly. A fine cast." He was lying on the couch, with the blinds drawn against the sun. "Want to watch with me? The showdown's coming up."

Penny had had enough showdowns for one day. "I've already seen it," she said.

"So have I. But I never get tired of it."

"Naturally, you don't." She held on to the back of a straight chair to steady her trembling hands. "That's because it's a fairy story."

"*High Noon*?" he asked, puzzled. "Are we talking about the same film? It's a western."

"The setting doesn't matter. It's still a fairy story. In real life, if all those gunmen were after one lone sheriff, he wouldn't stand a chance."

"That's where you're wrong."

"I give up on you," she cried, throwing up her arms. "Do what you like. Go to Timbuktu. To China. Maybe you can locate Aladdin's lamp."

Lon was quiet a long moment. "I can always change the channel if that's the way you feel about it," he said.

She squeezed her eyes shut, but the flood of tears came anyway. Holding her hand to her mouth didn't stop the shuddering sobs that came with them. In an instant Lon was cradling her. "I'm sorry about the house, baby," he said helplessly, when her weeping subsided. "God knows, I'm sorry. I'd give anything if I could get it back for you. It's gone. And all the money in the world couldn't change it back the way it was, even if I could buy it.''

"It isn't only the house," she said miserably.

"I know. You had hopes maybe you could get your mom and me back together. But that's only a dream. We were one hundred percent wrong for each other. She wanted me to be something I wasn't. I tried to fit her into the rootless life I wanted. It wasn't fair to either of us.''

"You need someone," she insisted.

"I have someone. Wanda's a terrific person. I think you could be friends with her if you'd give her half a chance. I've been standing back hoping it might happen if I didn't push it.''

"Wanda," she sighed. "I suppose you love her.''

"I suppose I do," he said haltingly.

Shots being fired in the television movie distracted her, and she turned toward it. The screen brightened and there was a close-up of Grace Kelly. She'd always reminded Penny a bit of her mother. She had the same regal kind of beauty. How could Wanda possibly compare favorably with Constance in Lon's eyes?

"I was somewhat disappointed, too," Her father sniffed and patted his sweater pocket for the handkerchief that wasn't there. Exasperated, Penny popped a tissue out of its box and handed it to him.

"Disappointed how?" she asked.

"I sort of hoped you and that college boy you were seeing would go to the altar. You would have made me a grandpa by now. And from what you wrote about him, you seemed good together.''

"Seemed?" Fuming, she turned away. She wasn't in a mood for defending herself and had no intention of going over the same ground she'd already been over with her mother. "We were ludicrous together," she said. "You can't know how it was between us. You only—" She broke off midsentence when she realized that her father was wearing a self-satisfied grin. He hadn't meant what he was saying. He was baiting her.

"You're right, baby. I can't know how it was." He clicked off the television. "You made me miss the big finale."

He was impossible. "I have to take a shower," she told him, as he started toward the kitchen. "And—" she hesitated a moment "—I love you."

"Me, too," he said, stopping to look at her. "So how about us letting each other breathe?"

She stared at him, uncomprehending. She had jeopardized her chances with Steffan because of him, and now he was accusing her of interfering.

She shut herself in her room, slipped out of her shoes and lay across the bed. The spread felt cool and soft beneath her. It was a handmade quilt done in autumn colors. The sort of quilt she would have liked to attempt for a bed she shared with Steffan. She'd never done any sewing other than a few high-school projects, such as pot holders and aprons, but after seeing Marissa's work and the love she put in every stitch Penny was besieged with the desire to try.

Steffan. "Don't ever pull away from me again," he'd warned.

Was it impossible for them to make a life together? Had their inability to come to an agreement and the ensuing blowup destroyed any hope of a reconciliation?

When she'd torn away from him, she'd been so blinded by her own certainty of what was right, she hadn't cared if she ever saw him again. Now she cared. Separation seemed unthinkable.

Though she'd settled down for a long period of soul-searching and feeling sorry for herself, she found it unnecessary. Steffan's reasoning made sense when she examined it calmly. If he went along on the next trip, watching out for her father, nothing disastrous could happen, could it?

Had Lon's brush with death really sobered him? Possibly, but she had her doubts. Would he agree to take more care in planning future expeditions? Maybe. But she'd believe that when she saw it. Would he turn author and put his experiences to good use? Also possible. The stories he told could fill ten books.

Should she give up the fight and allow him his chance at a super touchdown before this supposed reformation?

She smiled wanly. He'd take that chance anyhow, with or without permission. Someone else would supply the money if Steffan backed out. Someone who might turn out to be like those men who went with him to Peru.

In a few minutes she was on her feet, changing into a green-and-white print cotton dress that did something for her eyes, brushing her hair and adding a touch of mascara. She was preparing for the confrontation.

Steffan would still be angry, she was sure. But it would be impossible for him to look at her and remain that way. Hadn't Marissa said that making up was the best part of a relationship? Well, Penny would soon test the theory.

She groaned in frustration when, after flying into the house and down the corridor, she found the office empty.

The blinds were closed and the desktops were bare, except for a note requesting that she be at the downtown Korda Inn tomorrow morning at nine-thirty. There would be an important conference, and while it was in progress, Penny was to take some of the men's wives to see the sights. The note gave suggestions as to what should be on the agenda and where they should go for lunch.

"Wonderful," Penny said with a sigh.

It was going to be torment to wait for her own meeting with Steffan, to tell him how she felt and see his reaction. Where was he now? Would Wanda know?

The phone rang, and out of habit, she almost answered it. But the recorded message on the machine did the job for her, and she turned to leave.

"Penelope, sweetheart," Sonny Wheeler said, "just wanted to remind you about my party tonight. I'm looking forward to seeing you. The Hotel Markham. Suite fourteen sixty-eight. Be there."

"Don't hold your breath," she growled, closing the door behind her.

"Daddy?" she called, as she stepped onto the porch and heard a clatter inside the cottage.

"It's Wanda," came the answer. "Your pa's not here. Don't mind me. I'll be out of your hair in a sec." The woman was on her hands and knees, searching for something under the couch. "Have you seen the Nikko Minotis envelope? The map and the folder of documents?"

"Isn't it in the drawer?"

"If only it were." Wanda stood up and stuck a cigarette between her lips without lighting it. "I'm afraid to ask the next question."

Penny tried not to show her exasperation. She'd decided not to make any more protests against the upcoming treasure hunt, but she didn't intend to help with it. "Go ahead and ask."

"When Sonny came to pick you up the other night, did you, by chance, invite him in here?"

Sonny. Penny had heard as much about Sonny Wheeler as she cared to hear. "I didn't invite him in, exactly. He invited himself."

"Oh, lord." Wanda made a choking sound and sat down. "Did he see the map? Did he look at the folder?"

"No. That is . . . yes. What possible difference could it make? He wasn't interested."

"He was interested all right."

"Sonny is a wealthy man. He has a business to operate. Why should he bother with that nonsense?"

"Sonny is a shark." Wanda began to massage her temples as if she could rub away this new trouble. "He inherited the business. He signs a few papers and puts in a token appearance when absolutely necessary. But his trusted employees do all the work. Cutting throats is the greatest part of his fun. He's been in on a few deals with Lon, but . . . Oh, hell. Lon is going to kill me. I should have hidden those papers away somewhere. I just forgot."

Penny hardly heard Wanda. She was thinking back to the restless way Sonny had stalked the room, looking everything over. He'd unfolded the map, pretending it meant nothing to him, and like a fool, she'd even explained to him what it was.

"Couldn't Dad have stuck it safely away in a closet or drawer?"

"No way. We looked for it this morning. Then he said he figured you'd hidden it, hoping he'd forget the whole thing. You know, out of sight, out of mind."

"What about the maid?"

"Are you kidding? Lon is so protective of this place, he doesn't let anyone in to clean." She heaved a deep sigh that seemed to drain all her strength. "What am I going to say to him?"

"Maybe you won't have to say anything." Penny tried to remember if Sonny had been carrying anything when he left. He hadn't. But he could easily have slipped out to the car while she was dressing. "I doubt he's had time to act on anything yet. He'd be too busy making arrangements for a party he's having tonight."

"A party? How do you know?"

"He left me an invitation on the answering machine. I'm going to accept it."

Wanda blinked. "Do you think you should?"

"What choice do I have? My father will think I either gave those papers to Sonny or arranged for him to take them." She didn't add that after the way she'd fought her father's plan, Steffan would think the same thing.

"I'd offer to come with you, kid," Wanda said, frowning. "But I promised I'd pick up your dad in another half hour. We're supposed to go out to dinner with some friends."

"That's all right." Penny pictured Sonny's pink boyish face and the impish grin. What incredible nerve he had to call her after what he'd done. Did he believe his charm could make her overlook the fact that he'd stolen her father's papers?

She wouldn't have wanted Wanda to come with her, anyway. This was something she had to handle by herself.

It took self-control, but she wanted to wait until the party was in full swing before she arrived. That way she wouldn't have to be alone with him again. Throbbing music assailed her ears as she stepped off the elevator. Following the sound to his suite, she found the door ajar and entered without knocking.

The lights were dim. A man in a tuxedo was passionately kissing a woman who wore tight, knee-length jeans and a bare-midriff top. Her straight black hair, secured by a beaded headband, fell below her waist.

Although a vibrating stereo provided more than enough music, a woman in a caftan sat in front of the fireplace, strumming a guitar and singing something about faded photographs. A man seated beside her beat on bongo drums. The furniture had been pushed against the wall to make room for the few couples who had energy enough to dance. Sonny wasn't among them.

A streak of rosy light fell across a short hallway to her left, drawing her toward another room where she could hear a woman laughing. Mumbling excuses, she squeezed through a knot of people who were arguing hotly about the best place to get Thai food.

A hand gripped one shoulder and a wet kiss fell on the side of her neck. "You're late, sweetheart."

The sight of Sonny fanned the flames of her fury, and she had to struggle to keep from screaming at him. She didn't want to make a scene, though it was doubtful anyone would have noticed even if she'd set off firecrackers. "Late? How can I be late, when I had no intention of coming here at all?"

"Because I know you better than you know yourself. I didn't doubt it for a moment."

"That's probably true. When I received your invitation, I hadn't yet realized that you'd stolen something from me."

"Your heart, I trust?" Grasping her elbow firmly, he steered her down the hall, past the open door, to another room, this one with its door closed. He rapped with his knuckles on the paneling, listened, then turned the knob. "Party etiquette," he explained in a boozy voice. "You never know."

A lone woman stood on the balcony outside the room, sipping from a champagne glass and gazing out over the city. She wore a clinging, white satin gown, fashioned like something worn by Jean Harlow in the thirties. Her hair was white-blond like Harlow's, too.

She came in when she heard someone enter the room, and her mouth gaped when she saw Penny. "Who's she?"

"An old friend. Why don't you run along and get yourself a drink, honey?"

"I've got one."

Sonny's jaw squared. "Get another one. And close the door behind you." Circling her, he placed a hand firmly on each of her shoulders and pushed. "See you later."

She wriggled free with a curse, set her glass down so hard it should have shattered and fastened Penny with a look of sheer hatred before departing.

"You might regret you did that," Penny said tightly. "The business I have with you won't take long, and you'll wish you had the company."

He wasn't listening. Humming to himself, he strolled onto the balcony and held out his arm to her. "Come here, sweetheart. I want to show you something."

She almost laughed. Was he going to do the Franklin Lacey bit? "Do you imagine St. Louis is a city made up of log cabins? We have a tall building or two."

"I never took you for the farmer's daughter. Humor me." He wrinkled his nose in a way that was meant to be disarming. "Come here."

She moved stiffly onto the balcony and stood beside him. The night was starless and deep purple. The lights below were enchanting, but if they were supposed to provide a romantic backdrop for Sonny's clumsy line, they were wasted. A blackout would have been more helpful.

"Isn't this something?" He propped his elbows on the rail. "I like being high, looking down. Know what I mean?"

"No."

"Stand down there and what have you got? Bars, night-clubs, laundromats, all-night markets. Traffic snarls. Up here it changes. It's magic."

Penny folded her arms and looked up at him without trying to disguise her contempt. "Will you return my father's map to me now, or do I start searching for it?"

Sonny let his head drop forward and snorted. "You are one ding-a-ling lady. A pretty one, but a ding-a-ling nonetheless."

"Anything you say. The map, please."

"What map is that?"

"Obviously I mean the one you stole from the Korda guest house."

Sonny pushed himself away from the balcony rail. "The one I *stole*?"

"When I went into the other room to change, you slipped out to your car with it."

"Hell, yes. Along with a couple of ashtrays and your Aunt Matilda's silver soupspoon."

"Don't you scavengers have a code of ethics? I trusted you enough to—"

"Hold it right there, honey." He waved one hand to silence her. "I presume we're speaking of the treasure map I saw at your place?"

"Your presumption is correct."

He laughed and shook his head. "You seriously think I'd pack in everything here and sail off to some godforsaken island where there wouldn't be a good bar for miles? That I'd get suited up and drop into shark-infested waters? For what? Come on, now. You can think of a better excuse than that to pay me a visit. Not that you need an excuse. I don't have any hard feelings about our last meeting. It was kind of cute, you swinging that umbrella at my skull. I know the games females play. Not one in a hundred will come out and say, 'I dig you and you dig me. Let's make the most of it.'"

Sonny's voice rumbled on and on somewhere in a distant corner of her mind. The music was louder than ever. The walls seemed to move in and out with its throb. A woman's laugh, like a hen's cackle, echoed through it all. There was a crash and the shattering of glass and the woman laughed again.

The truth was plain in Sonny's pampered baby face, in his soft hands and in the way he had of breathing hard at the slightest exertion. He was no more a treasure hunter than she was.

She gripped the balcony rail as a fragrant breeze lifted her hair, brought her back to reality, and made her aware of her host, who was standing close behind her now. "I shouldn't have come," she said.

"Let's just say it was fate."

"Fate," she repeated. She turned and found herself in the circle of his arms. With a groan, she ducked under them. "Stop this nonsense. I'm in no mood."

"Protest noted and appreciated," he said through tight lips. "Now, where were we?"

She hadn't thought him capable of moving so fast. Maybe he hadn't. Maybe the sharp blow of realization had set her in such a foggy confusion, her own movement was slowed. But before she could note the sequence of steps, she was stretched out on the balcony's chaise longue, with Sonny over her, his mouth grinding into hers. The sour whiskey taste of his kiss turned her stomach, and his weight was crushing.

She heard the crash of the door, the roar of voices and the footsteps as the party overflowed its bounds and closed in around them. All at once, Sonny jerked away with a furious roar, and she sat up, choking and wiping at her mouth with the back of her hand.

"You bastard!" She heard Steffan's voice before she saw him.

The other guests, exhilarated by the possibility of a fight, formed a swaying, breathing barrier between the two men.

"What are you doing here?" Penny asked, rising to her feet. "How did you find me?"

Steffan was Siegfried ready to battle the dragon. Or was he the dragon? His face was distorted into a caricature of fury, his hands drawn into fists that might well have been lethal weapons. "Wait for me in the lobby," he snarled at her.

"But I have my own car."

He took a step toward her, his teeth clenched. "Do as I say."

"Come on, honey." The girl who'd been playing the guitar earlier put an arm around Penny's waist and began to guide her to the door. "The sooner you're out of here, the sooner this thing will dissipate."

"Choice advice, baby." A man with shoulder-length hair clapped a hand on her shoulder. "Do what your old man says, or there's gonna be bloodshed."

"Wanda," Penny whispered, as she rode down in the elevator.

It had been a setup. Wanda had sent her to Sonny's hotel for a map that wasn't really missing. Then she'd turned around and told Steffan where she'd gone, no doubt elaborating beautifully.

The pieces were beginning to fit snugly. Wanda had seen her put the swimsuit copy and sketches in the car the day she'd met Alex Zevos at the restaurant. When Penny went inside to check her appearance, Wanda had switched them with Steffan's environmental impact reports, figuring that if Penny looked incompetent she'd either quit or be fired.

The missing correspondence that day had undoubtedly been Wanda's doing as well. It would have been an easy matter for her to slip the letters into one of those disorganized-looking stacks of paper. And forgetting to mention that Garrett Wheeler called himself Sonny—had she *really* forgotten, as she'd claimed?

Penny could almost hear Wanda's laugh now, like the cackle of the woman at the party. It was a laugh of triumph.

As she waited in the lobby, she phrased and rephrased her explanation silently before the elevator doors finally parted to release a somewhat subdued but still grim-looking Steffan.

But when he clamped his fingers around her upper arm and steered her toward the revolving doors as if he were the hotel detective and she'd been caught rifling rooms, all explanations flew from her mind.

"Let me tell you how this happened," she began, once they were in his car. He'd insisted on driving her, despite her protests, muttering that he'd worry about picking up the Saab tomorrow.

"You're a big girl now, in charge of your own life."

This was going to be more difficult than she'd thought. "Wanda told you where to find me, didn't she?"

"Fortunately."

"But did she tell you why I was there?"

"Stay away from Wheeler," he growled, ignoring her queston. He hit the steering wheel with the flat of one hand. "I don't care where else you go or who you go with, but I'm asking—no, dammit, I'm ordering you—to stay away from him."

"You're ordering me?" Penny's heart beat out of rhythm. Maybe Wanda had done her a favor without meaning to. Maybe Steffan's jealousy would make him blurt out his feelings and declare himself. Up till now, he'd spoken to her of his need and his desire, but he hadn't said a word about love.

"On the surface he might seem very exciting," Steffan went on. "Everywhere he goes, people treat him like a king. He has more money than he could reasonably squander in two lifetimes, and he can be agreeable when he works at it. You might find him attractive. But he's shallow and unfeeling.''

She wanted to protest. Attractive? Exciting? *Sonny?*

But Steffan went on talking, even after she'd heard all she cared to hear and had stopped listening. She knew what he was saying, and love had nothing to do with it.

Her father was Steffan's friend. It always came down to that. Penny had met Sonny while working for him, and he blamed himself for the unpleasant consequences. That was all.

''You feel responsible.'' An ache pressed against her heart.

''Isn't that what I said?''

She pulled at a loose thread on her handbag. ''Then I suppose you'd be relieved if you were free of that responsibility. It would take the pressure off if I returned to St. Louis.''

He didn't hesitate. ''It would at that.''

''It's what you've wanted from the first.''

He didn't say any more. Penny stared out the side window, not wanting to look at his face, and not wanting him to see hers. He wouldn't have the satisfaction of seeing her tears. She'd cry in the privacy of her room.

CHAPTER THIRTEEN

THE FIRST RAYS of morning sun found Penny up and about with a good show, at least, of anticipation. She straightened the room she would soon vacate, called the airport to make travel arrangements, donned the same dress she'd been wearing when she arrived and packed her suitcase.

Her father wasn't as pleased about her decision as she'd supposed he would be. In fact he bellowed and paced the room when she told him of her plans, carefully omitting any reference to Steffan.

"You come all this way, say a few words to your old man, then poof, you're gone. I don't get it."

"I wanted to see you again. I saw you. Now it's time to go. I'm homesick."

"You said Greece was your home."

"It was. A long time ago."

"I don't buy that. Is it because of the house? Because I sold it? If it is—"

"A house is only a house—sticks and bricks and windowpanes," she chanted, almost meaning it.

"Then *I've* changed?"

She had to smile. "You'll never change."

"I can try." He smoothed a hand along his chin. "Just hang in there until this Naxos thing happens. You might think different about me then."

She took both his hands in hers. Never had she felt so close to him. "I love you, Daddy."

"Hell, I know you do. But maybe you'll respect me, too."

She caught her lower lip between her teeth. Her throat felt raw. "I do respect you."

His gaze was intense. "You wouldn't try to kid your old man, would you?"

When he went into the kitchen with his coffee mug for a refill, she escaped into the bedroom and closed the door. As usual, it was stuffy with the window shut. She sat at the dressing table and began combing her hair. A barometer of her moods, it was a cap of maddening tangles.

When someone tapped at the door, she dug her fingernails into her palms. The door inched open and she caught a flash of kelly-green blouse before she turned away.

"Want some coffee?" Wanda asked meekly.

"No."

"Thank you for not telling your father what I did. I know you've figured it out by now."

"It doesn't matter anymore."

"But it does. Lon's been walking on air, having you with him again. I tried not to see it. Now he's miserable, you're miserable, and I feel like a low-down jerk."

It was as it should be, then, Penny mused, unscrewing the top of her lip gloss.

"I'm not usually a devious person." Wanda sat on the edge of the bed and leaned forward, twisting her hands. "I didn't deliberately plot to drive a wedge between you and Steffan. I acted on a stupid impulse and believe me, please, I'd take everything back if I could."

That was easy to say now, since it was all over, Penny thought grimly. Deliberate or not, the result was the same.

"It came to me the day I misplaced the report and was worried how Steffan would react if I couldn't find it. He's such a perfectionist. You know how he flies off the handle when things go wrong, then apologizes later?"

"I know." Penny nodded. Considering his volatile nature, though, he'd been remarkably controlled in the face of her "inefficiency."

"You were typing away in the other room," Wanda went on, "and I thought, what If I did something to make him leap at your throat? You'd leap back, the fur would fly, and you'd leave in a huff."

"I might have. But I was determined to prove what a good secretary I could be."

"My... interference would have ended there, if it hadn't been for what you said to me in the garden."

"What did I say?" So much had happened in the past few days, Penny couldn't remember.

"You were going to try and take Lon back to St. Louis with you. Once he was there, you'd do your best to get him to stay. I was desperate. I couldn't imagine my life without him. If you and Steffan broke up, I thought, you'd go back where you came from and leave us in peace."

"You were right."

"I know." Wanda clasped her hands and brought them to her forehead. "If I'd had any idea how serious it was between the two of you, I wouldn't have acted the way I did. I would have warned you about Sonny—at least told you about his nickname. But it happened so fast, the thing between you and Steffan. I assumed it was simply a love-hate thing that would flare up and die out."

If only it had. Penny sighed, wondering as she looked at the woman's reflection in the mirror why she no longer felt any resentment toward her. What she felt instead was kinship. She could understand, even if she couldn't condone, Wanda's actions. Her love for Lon had driven her to do things she would never otherwise have done.

"I guess I'm as much to blame as you are," Penny admitted. "If I'd given you a chance, if we'd sat down together and talked it out, we wouldn't be having this conversation now. But there's something I don't understand. If you'd succeeded in driving me away, and my father had gone with me as I hoped, then where would you be?"

"If I acted quickly enough, before you really had time to work on him, it wouldn't have happened. He loves Greece. Wherever he goes, it's as if he can't take a really deep breath until he's back again."

"I know how he feels." Penny absently rubbed her hands along the surface of the glass-topped dressing table, trying to force back the wave of emptiness that spread through her at the thought of leaving the land she'd grown to think of as her home—and the man she'd grown to love so very much.

"Then there were the snapshots of your ma you kept leaving around for Lon to see. If you couldn't manage to lure him back to St. Louis, I was worried you might talk Constance into coming here for a visit. She's so beautiful, and she and Lon once shared so much. They might have got back together."

"Mother has what she wants in the States." Penny said, admitting to herself for the first time that Kenneth Glass probably wouldn't make such a terrible husband. That Constance might even love him. "She has security, a settled life, and a husband-to-be who'll come home for dinner every night."

"At the very least, if you stayed, you'd probably succeed in coming between your father and me. You disliked me from the first."

"I don't think my father would put you out of his life because of me," Penny said. She wouldn't tell the woman what Lon had said about loving her. That was something he'd have to do for himself. "And I didn't dislike you. Well...not really. I felt threatened by you. But inside, I was grateful you were here."

"How do you feel about me now?" Wanda drew a quivering breath. "After what I've done to you and Steffan?"

Penny thought for a moment. "Your plan wouldn't have worked if he hadn't been prepared to believe the worst."

"But he had his reasons," the woman tried. "He's distrustful of women anyway, because his mother abandoned him as a child, and because—"

"Because of the fiancée who betrayed him?"

"You know about that?"

"Marissa told me."

"That was what made my idea so perfect. You see, the girl was—"

Penny waved her hands. "I don't want to hear about it."

"But when you invited Sonny back here—"

"Please. No more. It doesn't matter now."

"There were no second chances," Marissa had said. "Steffan is unforgiving, like most Capricorns."

Penny wasn't a believer in astrology. She didn't buy the part about Capricorns. But the part about Steffan giving no second chances? That was another story altogether. Penny rose unsteadily to her feet, wanting only to end the conversation.

Wanda caught her arm as she started back into the living room. "Stay in Greece. Please. I'd rather lose Lon than see him so unhappy. It's another failure for him, don't you see? A failure that may be worse than all the rest. I'll go to Steffan, if it'll help, and explain the whole thing."

"It won't help."

"Will it help to run away?" Wanda shot back. *As your mother did,* she didn't add. But the words hung unspoken in the air.

Lon was still in the kitchen, moving about strongly now. His injuries were healing as quickly as if he'd been a much younger person. Maybe the fact that he'd never grown up was an advantage.

"What are you two jawing about?" he called.

"Good grief." Wanda wriggled her nose. "What's that foul smell?"

"I'm making a grilled cheese. Want one?"

"Good grief. Let me fix it for you."

"It's already done."

"Done and overdone. You can't eat that."

"Watch me."

Penny looked out the window at the miniature rose bush where she and Steffan had stood the morning before everything fell apart. She *was* running away, as Wanda had accused, doing exactly what she'd always blamed Constance for doing.

"Just hang in there until this Naxos thing happens," her father had said. "Maybe you'll respect me, too."

Did he believe that her respect for him depended on the success of his ventures? Had she made it seem that way?

Why was she leaving? Because the house was no more? A house was only sticks and bricks and windowpanes, wasn't it? as she'd told her father. If she was leaving because of Steffan, would distance make the pain of losing him easier to bear? Why should it? She loved Greece. It was where she belonged.

Why then?

"Who are you calling?" her father asked, when she picked up the telephone.

"The airport. I'm going to cancel my plane reservations."

"You're staying?"

"I'm staying," she said.

"That's my girl." He swooped over and wrapped his arms around her. She had to struggle to keep him from lifting her off her feet.

After she'd made her call, she went into the kitchen with him to keep him company as he finished his sandwich. Now that she'd gone this far, she thought, now that she'd committed herself to staying on and seeing everything to the end, whatever that end would be, she might as well commit herself all the way. Just this once, she'd give her father a vote of confidence.

"Steffan told me you're going to the islands in a few days. To discuss details of the Naxos venture and to see about a crew," she said.

Lon stopped eating and slid his tongue over his upper lip, tensing for battle. "And if I am?"

"I'd like to go, too."

He blinked. "Now, baby—"

"I won't interfere. I simply want to go along."

"Well . . ." He looked helplessly at Wanda, who only grinned back.

"Please," Penny begged.

"If you're sure."

"I am."

Wanda was at the sink, washing dishes left over from the previous night's snacking. Penny picked up a dish towel and began to dry. So her father had agreed to take her to the islands with him. But what about Steffan? When she'd told him she was leaving Athens, he'd readily agreed that it was a wise decision. How would he react to her change of heart? She wasn't eager to find out.

Until it was time to go, she'd stay close to the house and keep out of his sight. When they were on their way, it would be too late for him to object gracefully.

The days of waiting dragged, even though she kept busy. She called her mother, finally got through and listened dutifully to glowing stories about Kenneth. He had taken her dancing on the riverboat one night and had surprised her by being able to do the tango, the rumba, and half a dozen other intricate steps. He'd been taking dancing lessons in secret to please her.

"Can you imagine your father doing that?" she asked.

"No, I can't." Penny almost choked on the thought.

During her self-imposed confinement, she watched more television than she'd watched in an entire month before. Despite the storm of regrets that raged inside her, she managed to finish a series of drawings and copy lines she was certain Alex would approve. As usual, she did some of her best work under pressure.

Still, by the morning of their departure for the islands, she was ready to climb the walls.

Wanda had promised not to tell Steffan that Penny had remained in Athens. If she'd kept her promise, and he really didn't know, he was remarkably straight-faced when he saw her. He nodded, said a few courteous words and gave her a heart-tugging smile. His gaze didn't linger on hers, though, and nothing he said indicated that he'd wasted any of his time rethinking his own behavior.

His knit shirt, such a pale shade of yellow it was almost white, gave an appealing glow to his features. His hair, ruffled by the morning breezes, looked blue-black. Though she'd known he would be going on the trip, too, and had repeatedly rehearsed this moment—how she would smile, what she would say to mask her true feelings—Penny's stomach knotted at the sight of him. Her phantom self whispered in her ear, making her heavy-lidded with longing.

During the hours of driving that followed, Lon, keyed up about his plans, talked nonstop, and there were no uncomfortable silences. He'd spoken with Yuri Stravos the night before, he said, and Yuri was "in" for sure, ready to dig into his pocket for his share of the expenses.

"That way, nobody will lose too much if things don't pan out."

Penny exchanged meaningful glances with Wanda. It was the first time in her memory that her father had ever allowed himself to consider the possibility of failure. Maybe he *had* changed a little. Or maybe it was the first time he'd ever felt free to speak so openly.

"Yuri couldn't make the trip this time," Lon went on. "But he'll be with us on the big day, and he wants us all out to his place for dinner when we get back. Marissa will fix us something special to celebrate."

The ship they took was aptly called the *Melteme*, the Greek word for the wind that blew off the islands. It was especially strong today.

Wanda was deathly ill from the movement of the sea before they'd even been out an hour. She could only sit pale-faced and tight-lipped, now and then muttering to herself that she should have her head examined for not staying home. Lon sat beside her, comforting her with such gentle compassion that Penny wondered if he didn't welcome this chance for a turnabout. To take care of her for a change.

Spray from the sea struck her in the face so often, she no longer noticed it. Foolishly she'd chosen to wear a skirt, and to the entertainment of some of the watchful male passengers and crew, was kept busy trying to keep her legs covered.

People continually lost their footing as they moved about, and after a while stopped apologizing when they stumbled into each other. Deck chairs that weren't occupied flapped and tumbled everywhere.

Preoccupied by her efforts to preserve her modesty as she walked from one side of the ship to the other, Penny weaved off balance. Strong hands reached out to set her right and she mumbled her "thank you" before she realized her rescuer was Steffan.

"Better hold on to something," he advised, not offering his arm as that "something."

"I think I should."

"The *cambanatos*," he said, as they stood at the railing together.

"The wind that rings the church bells," she translated.

He looked down at her with a hint of a smile twinkling in his eyes. "I sometimes forget. You're almost as Greek as I am."

A student tour was on the same ship, adding to the choas. Mostly boys—though there were three or four girls—they drank soda pop, laughed, sang and danced to the loud music from the amplifier.

The bedlam made conversation difficult, which was just as well, Penny thought. The trite things they were saying to each other were not the things that should be said by two people who had shared what they had shared. But that part of their relationship was over, **wasn't it**? The remembrance filled her with raw despair.

At last Mykonos, the island designated as their meeting place, appeared. White stone, golden domes and windmills against gray-brown rock, it looked so much like a picture postcard that it added to her sense of unreality.

Georgie met them at the dock and, after greeting each with a vigorous handshake, scurried off to advise Nikko of their arrival.

Nikko looked as ferocious as before, though he wore a neat blue jacket with silver buttons and a fisherman's cap and had taken some pains to tame his hair and beard. With a thundering laugh, he clapped Steffan on the back so hard Penny couldn't understand why the younger man didn't fall to his knees. He even found it in his heart to favor Penny with a nod and a grunt, before crooking his finger for them to follow him to their quarters. They wouldn't be staying in the hotel.

"Too many tourists," he explained, pronouncing the word "tourists" as someone else might have said "snakes" or "spiders."

A kindly widow nearby offered rooms to rent for short stays, Nikko told them. Her house was clean and comfortable and quiet.

The streets were mazelike—twisting, turning and all the while climbing. It would have been possible for a person on one balcony to reach out and touch a person on the balcony across the way. Here was a steep ramp. There a group of shallow steps, hollowed by generations of feet. Then came a dead end, followed abruptly by another twist, and then steps climbed again between tall whitewashed stone walls, decorated in spots with tin cans of pink geraniums.

Nearby, Nikko had said?

"The streets were made so to foil pirates and roving marauders," Nikko explained, gesturing in a way to suggest the weaving path they followed. "There were a lot of them in the old days."

"I can see how it would work," Lon said, panting. "But what could they get that would be worth the effort?"

Penny was almost out of breath by the time they reached the red-painted door that allowed them entrance to a circular courtyard whose walls spilled over with more geraniums. A huge aviary filled with twittering birds sat in the center, and a woman with waist-length black hair was removing her wash from a line they had to duck under to get to the stairs.

Wanda walked like a windup doll, her eyes glazed, her feet barely leaving the ground. When they were shown to the room she was to share with Penny, she fell on the bed, groaning to be left alone to die.

Lon rushed downstairs again and came back with a glass of something fizzy that was supposed to help seasickness. But she was too miserable to take it.

"I'll see that she does," Penny promised, clasping his hand. "Don't worry."

"Would you rather go downstairs and have something to eat?" Steffan asked solicitously. "Or shall I make arrangements for someone to send up a tray?"

"Please don't anyone mention food until we get back to Athens," Wanda begged.

"Will you girls be all right?" Lon wanted to know.

"We'll be fine." Penny kissed him on the cheek. "Do whatever you need to do. We'll see you in the morning."

"Maybe not." Lon lowered his chin to his chest and scratched his head. "If the wind dies down, we're going to sail out as soon as it gets light. Just to have a look."

Penny bit her tongue to contain the comment she wanted to make. "Okay, then. We'll see you when we see you."

It was a small room, sparsely furnished. But it was clean and pleasant enough, with tall windows covered by gauzy curtains. A basin and candles sat on the dresser, the only piece of furniture besides the double bed. Religious pictures hung on the walls.

After waiting an hour to use what seemed to be the only bathroom, Penny took a hasty shower and washed her hair. She came back to the room to find that Steffan had sent up a tray after all. Spinach pie, a compote of spiced fruit and a piece of nutty sweet baklava. Though she thought she wasn't hungry, she ate almost everything, including Wanda's share, which would otherwise have gone untouched.

Someone was having a celebration at a nearby café. There was loud bouzouki music and laughing. When she looked out the windows she could see shadows along the wall; people appeared to be dancing through the streets.

The watching and listening made her remember earlier days, when Basil Korda was alive and used to hold frequent parties. Drawn by the music and laughter from the Korda villa, she would sit in her pear-tree perch, easily picking Steffan out of the crowd. Sometimes there would be colored lanterns making magic in her mind, and a small combo of musicians, and she'd concentrate with every particle of her being, trying to make believe that she was the girl in his arms.

She would imagine how he'd smile down at her. How she would smile back and toss her head becomingly, and he would draw her closer and whisper in her ear. The chill that ran through her had been real.

It had been wishful thinking then, and it was wishful thinking now. Had she been wrong when she made the decision to stay in Greece? Had she been foolish to come along on this trip? Would time, the proverbial healer of pain, also need distance to do its work in this case?

Instead of being annoyed by the din from the café, she welcomed it. Loud as it was, it couldn't equal the tumult in her heart. Sleep would not come easy.

CHAPTER FOURTEEN

SHE AWOKE EARLY to discover that Wanda had awakened even earlier, had found some coffee, and was back in bed again, half-asleep and unresponsive.

The wind had died down considerably which meant the men had probably gone out on the boats already. That wouldn't keep Penny cooped up. Though she didn't feel much like playing tourist, she'd never been on Mykonos before and felt obligated to go out and see what there was to see.

After dressing hastily in grass-green pants, a scoop-necked knit blouse with a green-and-white print, and a pair of comfortable sneakers, she tapped at her father's door. She was right. He had gone.

The same woman was downstairs at the clothesline, hanging articles this time, instead of taking them down. She smiled at Penny and nodded toward a door at the end of a short hallway.

"The gentleman is there," she said.

So her father hadn't left yet. Penny pushed the door the woman had indicated and found that it didn't lead into a dining room as she had expected, but into a garden.

An iron deer lay in one corner, half-hidden by a tangle of vines and wild flowers. An orange cat lay in a patch of sunlight at the feet of the garden's sole human occupant. The animal opened one yellow eye and yawned as Penny approached. Without announcing herself, she knelt to scratch the animal's scruffy fur, then glanced up at Steffan, sitting on the bench.

"Our landlady told me he's eighteen years old," he said, without registering surprise at seeing her. "He looks to be a veteran of many battles."

Penny did her best to appear casual despite the churning in her middle. "Isn't that terribly old for a cat?"

He nodded. "There's another, even older, crouching somewhere, watching us."

A tortoise lay dozing in the small circle of shade provided by an antique sundial, as red-winged grasshoppers played their games in the tall grasses. Nearby stood a fountain, fashioned of rough stones to look like a waterfall one might stumble upon in some wild place.

"I thought you'd be out to sea," Penny said.

"There was a problem with the boat. Nikko and Lon are working on it." He grinned crookedly. "I'm not much good in that department, I'm afraid."

Penny shifted from one foot to the other. "I'm not leaving," she said. "That is, I'm not leaving Athens."

"Why should you? The town's big enough for both of us." He drawled the words, as though he were reciting lines from a movie.

She dug her nails into the palms of her hands. If he cared about her at all, he wouldn't be able to speak so flippantly about her decision to stay.

"Exactly. I'll send home for some of the money in my bank account and get my own apartment. When the full-time job at Sun Dial is available, I'll take it." How was she able to keep her voice so steady, her words so clipped and sure?

"You didn't come into the office." His tone was a fraction rougher, reinforcing the accusation.

"When?"

"You were to show the visitors around the city, remember?"

"Oh, yes." It seemed so long ago. "Under the circumstances, I assumed you'd make other arrangements."

"I did. But I thought—" He broke off. "You might have finished off the week."

"I didn't think it would be wise."

The air between them fairly crackled with what was left unsaid. If she were to say she was sorry, would he say it, too, or would he berate her? Better not to pound the issue to death. He evidently came to the same conclusion. After a few moments, he relaxed visibly.

"Do you want to go somewhere and have breakfast?" he asked.

"No, thank you. I'm not hungry. I'd planned to take a long walk."

"Do you want some company?"

Did he expect her to refuse? Had he offered, hoping she would? Or was he fearful she'd wander off, as she had before, and foul up their schedule?

"Why not?"

As two of the three people closest to Lon, they would be thrown together many times in the months—the years—to come. They'd meet, talk casually about unimportant things and after enough practice, perhaps they'd stop feeling awkward together. But they had to start now.

When they were on the street, they looked at each other inquisitively, each wondering if the other preferred to go down to the waterfront, or to climb up on the rocks—to see the village as they passed through it, or to look down at it from above.

The decision was made without exchanging a word, and they began their ascent, beyond the man-set stones, to a path hammered out by donkeys' hooves. Now the scent of thyme was strong, along with a sweetish smell of smoke. In the distance they heard the sound of sheep bells.

Pebbles crunched under their feet as they stepped aside to allow an old woman, dressed entirely in black, to pass. She shook her cane at them, and Penny supposed at first she was scolding. But her words were friendly. She was only bidding them good-day.

When they were halfway up the mountain, they discovered a tiny church, partially hidden by shrubbery, withered thistle and oleander, and decided it was worth investigating. Though the church was barely furnished and plain inside, its wood was gilded and its icons were silver.

Larks shrieked at them as, with a sense of accomplishment, they reached the rocky pinnacle, and looked down at the little harbor with its forest of masts, backed by twisting whitewashed walls and little square cottages.

"Everything is so...so white," Penny said, flinging up an arm to shade her eyes. "It's almost blinding in the sunlight."

"Yes. It is," Steffan said with a kind of polite stiffness that told her his thoughts were elsewhere. "You believe you'll enjoy working for this...Alox?" He didn't look at her.

"Yes. He's a terribly nice man, and it's work I like."

"From what I've heard, he's everything he seems to be. He's honest and well respected in the industry."

Penny looked at Steffan sideways. "From all you've heard?"

"I did some checking after I saw you two at lunch." He shrugged. "I didn't want you getting involved with the wrong sort of man."

Involved? One lunch? "You mean, you didn't want Lon's daughter getting involved."

"Isn't that what I said?"

"No."

"And Wheeler?" He still wasn't looking at her. "Where does he fit into your plans?"

This was too much to ignore, even for the sake of keeping peace. "He doesn't," she snapped. "If we're going to be civilized about all this, don't throw that obnoxious clod in my face again. As if I couldn't do a hundred times better. No woman with an ounce of sensitivity would want to be in the same room with him."

Too casually he touched a finger to a place between his eyebrows and rubbed. "You were in the same room with him that night."

"Not by choice."

"He brought you there at gunpoint?" A muscle in his jaw twitched.

His sarcasm worked like a floodgate being opened, allowing all the outrage she'd felt at being accused without a fair hearing to rush forth. "When I tried to explain, you wouldn't listen."

"I'm listening now."

"It's too late." After so long, explanation seemed futile. It might only set the stage for another, even more bitter argument that would leave her crushed. If he had so little trust in her, he'd believe what he wanted to believe, anyway.

When she started to walk again, he fell into step beside her, though there was really only room for one on the path. Stooping down, he gathered a handful of pebbles and tossed them absently. His face was all planes and hollows, his bronzed skin taut, his dark eyes shadowed. "You said no woman would ever see anything in Wheeler."

Why wouldn't he let go of it? Clearly his antagonism and rivalry with Sonny Wheeler was a large factor in his bitterness. He didn't intend to lose out to the man in anything.

"I said it and I meant it."

"A girl I knew—a girl I thought I loved—saw enough in him to..." Steffan dropped the rest of the pebbles at his feet. "Well, Wheeler was the reason for our breakup. That's why I couldn't think clearly when I saw you with him. When I saw it happening all over again."

A girl I thought I loved, he'd said. A girl he *thought* he loved.

Wanda had tried to tell her something more about Steffan's fiancée, but she hadn't wanted to hear.

"Sonny Wheeler?" She stopped walking and stared at him in disbelief. "Did you give *her* a chance to explain?"

"Explain?" Steffan's laugh was more of a growl. "The scene I came upon in the cottage needed no subtitles to be understood."

The cottage. So that was what Sonny meant when he told her he'd been there before. This woman, whoever she was, had chosen to dally with an oaf like Sonny, when she could have had Steffan? The idea was incomprehensible to Penny.

"She must have been out of her mind," Penny gasped, thinking aloud.

"How do you mean that?"

Dear, dear Steffan, she thought. Could a man who had acquired a string of luxurious hotels in all parts of the world and run them as easily as another man might play a game of Monopoly truly be so unsure of himself when it came to love? Was it possible that he hadn't guessed how much he meant to her?

"What do you think I mean?" she asked, looking up at him not with the starry eyes of the child who'd adored him, but with the accepting eyes of the woman who loved him.

The phantom Penny, the one she usually kept in check, restrained by the confines of "proper" behavior, was threatening to step forward. To close the distance between her and Steffan. To slide her arms around his neck and pull his head down so she could breathe a feathery kiss here, there and here again. And then to allow herself the spell-binding pleasure of bestowing a kiss that would fill her with the intoxicating taste of him.

Sensing a change, Steffan narrowed one eye. "First tell me why you went to Wheeler's party."

What a strong and decisive mouth he had, yet how soft and yielding. With effort, she focused her thoughts on his question. Wheeler's party. "I thought Sonny had stolen my father's treasure map from the guest house. I went to his suite to get it back."

The line between Steffan's eyebrows deepened. A tempest still raged in his eyes. He wasn't convinced. "What the hell would Wheeler want with a treasure map?"

Penny grinned foolishly. "I thought he was another of your everyday ruthless scavengers."

"He's ruthless, all right. But the only treasure he'd bother diving for would be the olive at the bottom of a martini."

"I know that. Now." She began walking again. "You can believe it or not. It's true."

"I suppose I believe it," he said almost grudgingly.

"You suppose?"

He held up both hands in a gesture of surrender. "I believe it. Now tell me what you meant when you said my fiancée must have been out of her mind."

His tone told her he knew exactly what she meant. Directly in their path stood a huge rock, as though an obliging giant had placed it there for the use of overenthusiastic hikers. Penny leaned against it, and Steffan settled beside her.

"Well?" he persisted, not to be put off.

Pride be hanged, she decided. It was time to commit herself all the way. "I meant that I love you too much to imagine any woman willingly giving you up—or even looking at another man."

He exhaled loudly, as if he'd been holding his breath as he waited for her answer. "Oh, Sparrow." He reached for her gently but firmly, drawing her away from the rock to hold her at arm's length, opening and closing his fingers as though to reassure himself the moment was real. "If only you knew how much I've needed to hear that. You're so unpredictable. So distant at times."

"*I'm* distant? You sometimes acted as if you hated me."

"Did I?" Concern shone in his eyes. "It was only that I was afraid of you."

"Afraid?" It was hard to imagine Steffan afraid of anything.

"I can take financial setbacks and disappointments. Money lost can be made up again. But where love is concerned, when someone carries away a chunk of my soul, the emptiness doesn't fill up again so easily."

Love. He'd mentioned the word in passing and it lay there, insinuating, teasing, implying. But implication wasn't enough. Not now. "Go on," Penny prodded.

His eyes were velvet. The message she read there made her shiver. "Don't you know how I feel?" he asked. "Doesn't it show?"

She touched a finger lightly to the pulse throbbing at his throat. "Don't show me. Tell me."

He moistened his lower lip with his tongue. "I love you."

Her heart began to hammer crazily. "Completely?"

"Completely," he repeated. "I have, almost from the moment you arrived."

"And you were willing to send me away? To never see me again?"

"I expected you to come back to the office the next day and we'd have it out."

"And when I didn't?"

"I would have come after you, even if it meant nothing more than another of our knock-down-and-drag-out fights."

"Our finest moments have come after those fights," she said, devouring him with her eyes.

"I was all set to drive out to the airport to bring you back, but then Lon told me you'd changed your mind about leaving."

"You knew I was coming on this trip then?" No wonder he hadn't shown any surprise.

"Are you kidding? Lon told the maid, the cook, the gardener. I wouldn't be surprised to hear he stopped strangers on the street, he was so pleased. 'My little girl is with me on this one,' he told me. 'How can I miss?'" Steffan grinned. "If you're going to keep encouraging him this way," he teased, "how are we ever going to reform him?"

"The answer is, we're not," Penny said, only half-joking. Steffan's smile was wonderful. It warmed her from her breeze-tossed curls to the toes of her sneakers. Without thinking about the consequences of her actions, she grasped a handful of his shirt and gave a small tug, bringing him closer. "Now that you've told me how you feel about me," she said, when he looked surprised, "you can show me."

"Why you brazen little..." He laughed, an unreserved laugh this time, and with dizzying speed, spun her around and placed her flat on the rock, so that she was lying like an ancient sacrifice to the gods. In another instant, he had swung himself up to stretch out beside her.

"I didn't have to leave," she whispered, a split second before his mouth descended on hers, warm and gentle, erasing from her conscious mind all she'd wanted to say to him. She didn't want to think beyond this kiss, beyond the next, or the next after that. Only what was happening now, at this moment, mattered.

In sweet accompaniment, his throbbing fingers drifted through her hair, smoothed the side of her face and glided over her shoulders, exploring, yet hesitating and holding off inches from the thrusting breasts that cried for his caress.

Somewhere between the miraculous first meeting of their mouths, and the fourth—or perhaps the fifth, she'd lost count—he'd moved so close beside her, she could feel his ragged breathing, feel the heat of his damp skin beneath his shirt.

Then he pulled suddenly away from her. "It'll have to be soon," he said, grimacing as if in pain.

It will be, she thought deliriously, whatever "it" might be. Here in the lemon-colored sunlight, with thyme-scented breezes ruffling her hair, the tinkle of sheep bells in the distance, and reality more unreal than fantasy itself, she was ready to agree with anything he said.

Lying beside her on the rock, he folded his hands behind his head and looked up at the sky. "Zevos will have to do without your services. You owe us your loyalty."

"Us?" she questioned, raising on one elbow to gaze down at him.

"Korda Inns. I'll see that you get brochures and literature telling you about the history of the Wayfarer. You might even want to visit it. Then you can get busy on a campaign for its grand reopening, under new ownership, right away."

She traced the line of his cheekbone with one finger, excited by the idea, but too filled with lazy contentment to react to it. "You're offering me a job?"

"I am." He caught her hand and pressed his lips to the pulse point of her wrist. "How does a lifetime contract sound?"

"It'll do for a start," she said softly, wondering if he was saying what she hoped he was saying.

"If you have no objections, I'd like us to be married in Athens, at the villa."

Married. The sound of the single word set her heart to beating crazily again. She would have had no objections to their being married right now, right here where they stood.

"I think it would be perfect," she said. A small giggle escaped her lips before she could suppress it.

"What's so funny?"

How could she explain?

Long ago, as she'd sat in her pear-tree perch, she'd pictured herself in a white gown of satin and lace. She'd been standing beside an achingly handsome Steffan on the flower-filled terrace of the Korda villa. The scene had been so clear, she could almost hear the marriage vows. She'd felt him lift the veil and felt the pressure of his lips as he bestowed his first kiss on the lips of Mrs. Steffan Korda.

Her mother had been in her vision, weeping into a handkerchief. Her father had been there too, sniffing to control his own tears.

Now, oddly enough, it would happen exactly like that.

No. Not exactly.

Her mother would be there with Kenneth. Her father would be there with Wanda. They'd both found someone who loved them exactly as they were. Somehow that made truth more exciting and wonderful than the long-ago dream.

The thought of it filled her with intense joy, and she bent down to place a brief kiss of her own on the lips of the wonderful someone she herself had found.

"Mmmm." Unwilling to accept her small offering as final, Steffan caught her arms, pressing her back against the rock, and kissed her soundly.

But the kiss that started out with such passion stopped too abruptly. Or was it her imagination? She opened her eyes to see the old darkness jolt into his face.

"Wait a minute here," he growled. "What the hell was Wheeler doing at the cottage in the first place? How could he have taken the map?"

"I . . ." It struck her all at once that though she'd been blameless, his suspicions were beginning to make her feel and act guilty. Another small laugh quivered inside her and grew with his increasing consternation until she couldn't hold back.

He didn't see the joke. His eyes pierced hers and he gave her a small shake. "What was he doing there?"

Her words spilled out along with her giggles, until she had unfolded as best she could the story of the mishandled message and her determination to make good as his Girl Friday.

"That tale sounds more farfetched than the first one." He looked drained, but not angry or resentful. He thrust his fingers through his hair. "If I were to tell you such a story, if our positions were reversed, would you believe me?"

She thought for a long moment, trying to be entirely objective as she imagined how she would react if she were to come upon Steffan in the arms of another woman. It was too painful. Quickly she shook away the picture.

"I would have to trust you," she said. "Love is built on trust. However...from then on, I'd never let you out of my sight."

"Never?" he repeated.

"Never."

"Sound advice," he said, as he lowered his mouth to hers again. "And I believe I'll take it."

Six exciting series for you every month... from Harlequin

Harlequin Romance
The series that started it all

Tender, captivating and heartwarming...
love stories that sweep you off to faraway places
and delight you with the magic of love.

◆

Harlequin Presents
Powerful contemporary love stories...as individual as the women who read them

The No. 1 romance series...
exciting love stories for you, the woman of today...
a rare blend of passion and dramatic realism.

◆

Harlequin Superromance®
It's more than romance...
it's Harlequin Superromance

A sophisticated, contemporary romance-fiction
series, providing you with a longer,
more involving read...a richer mix of complex plots,
realism and adventure.